WICKED UNION

SARA MCCLAFLIN

First Edition

ASIN: B0FC5QHC72

ISBN (trade): 979-8-9914135-9-6

Book Cover: Pia

Editing: Brandy Gibson

Social Media: Tawny Gratto & Ashley Sullivan

PA: Sarah Toon

Marketing & PR: Wildfire Marketing Solutions

Content Warning

This book contains mature content and situations intended for adult readers (18+). Some of the events, conflicts, or character backstories may touch on sensitive topics.

Reader discretion is strongly advised.

If you'd like to see a detailed list of possible triggers and content notes before you begin, I've prepared one for you on my website: https://www.authorsaramcclaflin.com/wicked-union

Author Note

Liora and Evander weren't supposed to be more than a moment.

They showed up in *The Devil's Canvas* to flirt, tease, maybe raise a few eyebrows—and that was supposed to be it. A fun aside. A wink to the readers.

Then you started asking about them.

Who were they? What happened between them? How did they fall in love?

I couldn't stop thinking about it either.

Their story is one of hope and freedom. Where two people take a chance—not just on love, but on becoming something more. On grieving what was lost and rejoicing in what was found.

Liora and Evander's journey reminded me that the most subtle of bonds are sometimes the most unbreakable. That love doesn't need to roar to be real. Sometimes, it just needs to endure. To choose. To stay.

So thank you—for reading this novella, for asking for more, for loving them enough to want their story in full.

Their story wouldn't exist without you.

And honestly? I'm so glad it does.

Contents

The Demon's Oath

A Sacred Vow of Binding and Judgment

By the Depths of the Abyss, by the Shadows That Watch, by the Chains of Fate that no force may sever–

Let it be written. Let it be known. Let it be sealed.

I, **Evander Duvain**, of my own will and without coercion, do stand before the Unseen Council and swear this Oath, binding my existence to the Eternal Laws of Bargains, Punishments, and the Seven Sins.

I take upon myself the mantle of **Deal Maker and Deliverer of Judgment.**

I wield not the sword, but the contract, for a promise is sharper than any blade.

I wield not chains, but consequence, for a choice freely made is a fate unchangeable.

I wield not force, but inevitability, for what is agreed shall come to pass, no matter the pleading.

I walk among mortals not as a savior, but as a test–**to tempt, to offer, and to take.**

Thus, before the **Shrouded Thrones and the Abyssal Hosts**, I inscribe my vow into the **Book of Binding**, knowing that once my name is burned into these pages, my path is set.

THE LAWS OF THE OATH

I. The Deal is the Beginning.

To speak is to shape. To offer is to bind. Once my words seal a deal, there shall be no undoing, no regret, no escape.

II. The Bargain Holds Weight.

What is given shall not be returned. What is promised shall not be denied. No mortal, angel, or demon shall unravel the contract once it is set.

III. The Cost Shall Match the Desire.

Each soul shall be measured, and its burden weighed. The greater the sin, the greater the consequence. No deal shall be granted without its proper price.

IV. The Collector Does Not Pity.

I shall not sway, nor shall I falter. I shall take what is owed in its due time. No tears, no pleas, no prayers shall alter fate.

V. The Soulmate is Fate, But Duty is Eternal.

If I should find the one who bears my mark, the soul bound to mine by fate, I shall not deny them, for fate cannot be rewritten. To love is not a sin, but to forsake my duty for love is unforgivable.

Though my soul may recognize its other half, my purpose remains unshaken. I shall not waver, nor shall I allow this bond to weaken the will I have sworn to uphold.

If I place my soulmate above my duty, if I let them turn me from my path, then let my name be burned from the Abyss, my power stripped, and my soul cast into the void, lost to both fate and eternity.

VI. The Unseen Council Holds the Final Word.

Though their presence is unknown, their law is absolute. No punishment shall be given beyond what is agreed, and no deal shall be struck that defies the Balance.

VII. The Reckoning Shall Always Come.

No bargain shall go uncollected. No debtor shall go unpunished. In pain or in ruin, in torment or in nothingness—the price shall be paid.

SO IT IS WRITTEN.

SO IT IS SEALED.

SO IT SHALL BE.

SIGNED IN BLOOD AND HELLFIRE BEFORE THE UNSEEN COUNCIL

Evander Duvain

Signed in Blood, Marked by the Shadows, Sealed in Fire

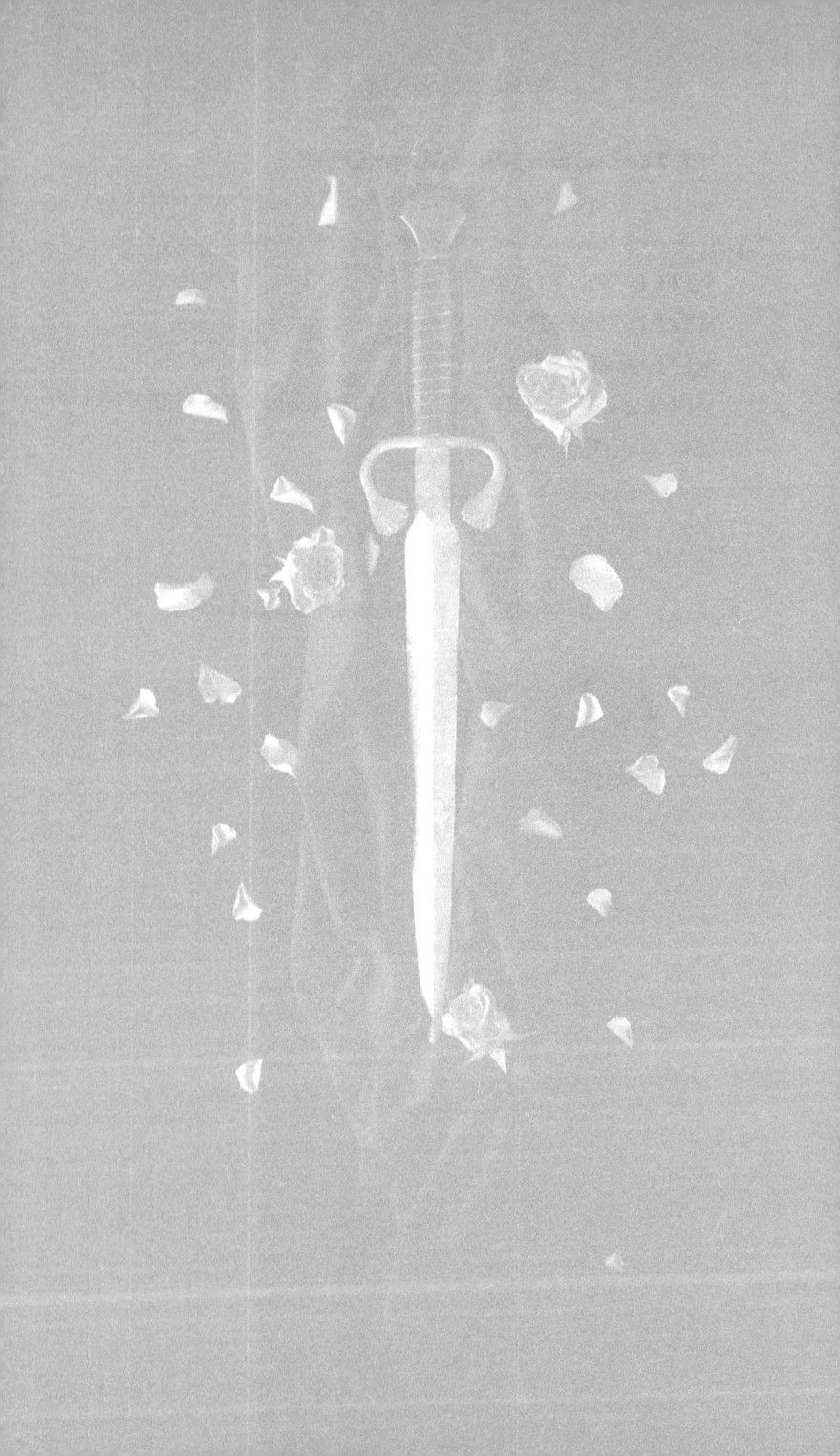

Chapter One
Evander

Paris thrives in late spring. Carriages crowd the streets, the air thick with roses, wine, and ambition. A pleasant shift from Hell's constant heat—though no less cutthroat.

Fashion, however, remains its own punishment. I prefer leather and steel—garments meant for work. But in high society, I endure silk stockings, petticoat breeches, and enough lace to smother a man. Power demands a uniform. Unfortunately, sometimes that uniform involves ruffles.

My parents refused to wear it. Cassian and Serenya Duvain never bowed to anyone. Not the High Court, not the old powers that fed on fear. They chose defiance over diplomacy, and it got them killed. My brother, Theron, was closer to them. I never understood what they were so angry at. Now I do.

Immortality freezes you somewhere between your mid and late twenties. Strength at its peak, beauty unspoiled by time—the perfect image to wear for eternity. My parents never lived long enough to see their faces settle. Theron stopped aging at twenty eight. I was twenty six. We look the same now as we did the day they died.

It's well past midnight when I reach the summoner's estate. Large enough to impress, ostentatious enough to betray desperation. The kind of house built to be admired from a distance—stone, manicured gardens, and every window blazing with candlelight as if to scream wealth into the night.

Beyond the gates, Paris lives in want. Families stacked in narrow rooms, the stink of refuse clinging to the streets. Inside these walls, they drink wine older than the men who pour it.

1719, and mortals still believe excess is the same as power. They build monuments to themselves while the city beyond starves—dressing their vanity in silk.

I portal straight upstairs to see a study with gold coating nearly every surface and useless trinket. Opulence at its best. They don't even look up, which is a grave insult.

I clear my throat.

"One second," the older man says. "My son and I are just discussing our plan."

"I don't have all night," I respond. I'm going to leave if they don't figure their shit out fast. "Decide or I'll find someone else who wants the opportunity."

"We want to talk about something," the younger one says.

"And that is?" I lift a brow. I'm intrigued now.

"We want to make a deal," the older guy says.

Mortals and their deals. It's why I'll never be out of a job—ambition outpacing their caution every time. They never think about the consequences. Only immediate gratification.

"We want a place among the King's circle," the young one says.

"I think we need a proper introduction before we go further," I say. "I'm Evander Duvain. You both are?"

The elder clears his throat.

"Philippe François de Launay," he says, cutting off his father.

He glances at the older man beside him. "And my father, Étienne."

I squint my eyes at them. The names mean nothing to me. Which I suspect is the reason they want to make this deal in the first place.

"Why do you think that the King would care for your company?" I tilt my head at them. This should be interesting to say the least.

Philippe glances at his father before answering. "Our family has...resources. But gold alone doesn't open the right doors."

"That is true," I say, walking closer to where they are seated at the desk and take the spare seat across from them. "Wealth is easy compared to status. But I can arrange your relationship with the king. Make the Launay name fashionable—envied even. For a price of course."

Étienne's mouth tightens. "That price?"

"When I come to collect," I say smoothly, "you will give me the most valuable thing your house possesses. Without hesitation. Without question."

Philippe smirks, as if it's a clever joke. His father just nods, too blinded by the promise to hear the warning.

"Do we have a deal?" I ask.

"Yes," Philippe says. "We do."

The contract appears in my hand with a thought—parchment older than their bloodline, the ink shimmering faintly, it already knows their names. I slide it across the desk.

They read. Their eyes widen. Every term is exactly what they want. So perfect it's dangerous. They don't even glance at the final clause. No one ever does.

When they nod, I call my dagger into being.

I take the sheath off, catch each of their hands in turn, and draw the blade across their palms. Not deep—just enough. Blood falls in bright drops onto the parchment. It sizzles, sealing itself into the fibers, before vanishing entirely. The ink darkens. The deal is done.

"The deal is complete," I say.

"What will happen next?" Étienne asks.

"You will marry into royalty. Don't ask me who because I don't know. Fate will guide you. Most likely you'll get a summons. Your son will marry and you're in," I say, sliding the contract into my coat.

I rise as they stand. They can't be the ones sitting while I'm standing. It makes them vulnerable. They think they're in charge.

I portal to the alley around their house. The humidity is still circling me as I think back to something my father always said.

"Power is a door, Evander. But you only walk through when they invite you in."

It's ironic that he always said things like that. He and my mother never waited for an invitation. They forced the door. I learned that's not always the best approach.

An hour later, I'm standing on the steps of the Palais-Royal district, where high society refuses to sleep. Carriages pull up to the arcades, spilling out men in embroidered coats and women draped in silks. The street is lined with hundreds of lanterns. The smell of perfume whips around me.

Music drifts from an open salon window, laughter spilling into the street that sounds like a coin hitting cobblestone.

This is the Paris the Launay family wants to be part of. Not in their studies late at night working, but not having to worry about anything.

"Did you hear about the Duchesne daughter?" A woman giggles.

"No," another says.

"Rumor has it her father chose a groom for her," she says.

"Finally. She's getting old, it's almost past her time to be married," another woman chimes in.

"At nineteen, I was already pregnant," the first woman says.

"Liora, a bride. Can you believe it?" The women all laugh like a gaggle of hens.

It's their favorite pastime. Always talking about marriage or children.

A tightness grips my chest—an unwelcome pain. I've felt it before. It's always fleeting and always empty.

I want what my parents had. Not their defiance, but their desire to work together.

My father was born a demon. My mother was not. She bore the Mark. A very specific one. Our family crest. The mark of Duvain.

It was more than just love. They were tethered together—body and soul.

I've waited centuries to feel the mark brand itself on my skin. Centuries all lead to nothing.

I think about the women. The woman that they were speaking of. Liora. It lands heavier than it should, settling somewhere deep.

A beautiful name. Wasted, most likely. Few marriages in this city are anything but political arrangements.

The men drift off into the crowd, their voices swallowed by the Paris midnight pulse. I turn back toward the Palais, but the name stays with me, as stubborn as a stone in my boot.

Chapter Two
Liora

I groan as heat spills across my face, light pressing against my closed lids. The curtains are pulled back, forcing me to hide my face under my pillow.

"It's time to rise, my lady," my personal maid says. "Your father wants to speak with you at first meal."

I bury my face even deeper into the pillow. If I don't move, perhaps I can delay the inevitable of learning the name that will bind me in a loveless relationship for the rest of my life. But time has officially run out.

I was at the Palais-Royal district last night. I heard all of the women talking. *Pity. Spinster. Such a shame. Waste of a woman.* As if being unmarried at eighteen is some grave deformity. Something must be wrong with the poor Duchesne daughter.

I knew this day would come. I never feared marriage—only the life they expect me to conform to with it. Endless luncheons, suffocating parlors, standing with my husband as we smile at men and women who judge my worth by my dowry and status.

I want a partner, not a warden. Fidelity, not political gains. And I know I will not find it in the bed of an aristocrat.

My maids descend on me like a flock of doves the minute that I stand up. They push me to my dressing table in the corner of the room.

It's like a small kingdom of its own—crystal bottles lined like soldiers, silver boxes holding powder as fine as snow, a mirror that shows every little line on my face.

Yvette, my head maid, is already getting my dress ready. She has been with me since my birth. Her son is my age and works as a butler at our estate.

She slips a silk shift over my head, the cool linen brushing on my shoulders.

"Hold still," she murmurs, putting on my corset. She starts to draw the strings as tight as they go. I hate this part. My ribs protest as my breath catches. She doesn't loosen it. Never does.

The hoops come next—two wide ovals of whalebone that open up my hips like a sail. The petticoat swishes over them like water over rock.

The gown she chose for me is my heaviest one. It's gold threaded covered in silk brocade that gleams. This is about making a stance.

Yvette pins the jeweled stomacher in place and all the ribbons are being tied. By the time she is finished, I can barely move.

"Too tight?" She asks without looking up.

"Always," I mutter.

She gives me a faint smile, tucking the last ribbon through its loop. "You said the same thing when you were twelve, wearing your first stays. You survived then and you'll survive now too."

"That one didn't come with a lifetime sentence," I say.

"A lifetime of comfort and influence," she corrects. "Not every woman gets to marry into a family that can offer them that. You'll be a duchess and your husband a duke."

I don't say anything because she is right. I should be grateful for the life I lead. Many are not as fortunate. I see them when I go to the orphanage. Children left there all alone and many starved.

Yvette smooths my skirts one last time. "Your parents are waiting."

The walk from my chambers to the breakfast room feels longer than usual. Servants dart out from corridors, carrying massive bouquets of flowers. The entire estate hums with preparations.

I'm the only child of the Duchesne family. And a daughter at that. My marriage is going to be an event of its own.

When I step into the room, my father is already seated at the head of the table with a half empty cup of coffee in front of him.

"Your mother is in the ballroom with the florists," Yvette says, a smile tugging at her lips. "She's been at it since dawn. I've never seen her so particular about roses."

I sit at the table as my father looks up from the court papers he was reading. "Liora, you're eighteen now. We held back as long as we could, but I think it's time that you marry. Society expected it already. Your mother and I decided on Philippe François de Launay. You'll meet him properly today." His voice is emotionless has he delivers the most earth shattering news of my life.

"I've never heard the name," I say, trying to keep myself calm, my tone even. I thought my family would want me to be with a man in court, not a random person. Either way, this is not how I wanted to start my day.

"That's good. He comes from a good family. He has no known enemies, no scandal, no debts to speak of. He comes from a family that produces gold bars. Wealthy people," my father says. The words sound practiced—like something he's recited a dozen times before. He doesn't look at me. Just turns back to his reading. I'm dismissed, not with cruelty, but with indifference.

A plate is set in front of me holding a small brioche, half a boiled egg, and some strawberries. My favorite meal.

I eat slowly, more for ritual than actual hunger. My father speaks of politics between sips of coffee. By the time the last strawberry is gone, my fate is sealed.

"The guests are gathering," he says, rising from his chair. "It's time."

We walk through the long marble corridor toward the dais. The air smells faintly of beeswax and roses, and the sound of voices swells with each step. Yvette fusses with my skirts as we approach the side door to the ballroom.

Philippe François de Launay is already waiting there, dressed in pale blue silk embroidered with silver thread. His wig is immaculate, every curl powdered into submission.

"Mademoiselle Duchesne," he says with a smile that doesn't quite reach his eyes.

"Monsieur de Launay," I reply, dipping my chin.

"I've been rehearsing a passage from Virgil for the occasion," he says, adjusting his cuffs. "I find Latin lends a certain... gravitas to these moments."

"I'm sure it does," I answer, keeping my tone polite even as my stomach knots.

"*Fortune favors those who dream.*" He smiles, clearly pleased with himself.

I arch a brow. "*Fortune sides with him who dares.*"

His smile falters for half a second before returning. "Ah. Yes. That's what I meant."

Of course it is. It always is—whatever I say, whatever he hears, it must align. Because he cannot fathom being wrong.

"Naturally," I say, my voice flat, letting the word hang in the air just long enough for him to feel it.

He doesn't notice. Or maybe he does and chooses to ignore it. I'm not sure which stings more.

The herald raises his voice, announcing our names to the crowd beyond the door. Philippe offers his arm. I take it, because there is no choice, and we step into the light together.

"Mademoiselle Liora Duchesne and Monsieur Philippe François de Launay — betrothed in union, blessed by fortune and the crown!"

Applause swells like a tide, drowning out my own thoughts. The chandeliers glitter overhead, casting fractured light across faces flushed with wine and self importance.

Philippe stands tall beside me, accepting bows and congratulations with a smile practiced in mirrors. He's basking in the attention. Something he has clearly never had before.

I keep my smile where it belongs. On my lips, not in my eyes. Yvette calls it grace.

This is not the type I thought my father would ever choose for me. Someone so below us. I'm not saying that it's a bad thing. I don't care. But his shoes don't fit right and everything feels to be very superficial.

My father shakes Philippe's hand, their eyes meeting in silent agreement over the bargain I've just been folded into.

I wonder if anyone in this room can see the bars.

To them, it's a ballroom. To me, it's a cage with golden hinges.

"*Ma fiancée,*" he says smoothly, offering his arm. "As Virgil said—*Amor vincit omnia.*"

"And yet you left out the first part," I reply, slipping my hand into the crook of his elbow. "*Omnia vincit amor; et nos cedamus amori.* Love conquers all; let us, too, yield to love."

His smile falters for half a second before snapping back into place. "Ah, yes. I preferred the shorter version."

"Most men do," I say lightly. The guests laugh, thinking it a jest. He squeezes my hand—just enough to sting—and steers me forward through the crowd.

My smile stays fixed, but inside, I'm already counting the ways this cage could be broken.

We make our rounds of handshakes, greetings, and thank you for comings. Philippe basks in it all, his laugh perfectly timed, his titles rolled out like treasures.

The moment the last well wisher turns away, his grip on my arm tightens.

"A word of advice, ma fiancée," he says, voice smooth but just tight enough for me to hear the edge. "When I quote Virgil, you smile. You do not correct me."

I arch a brow. "When you quote Virgil correctly, I'll consider it."

His smile doesn't reach his eyes. "You'll find marriage is easier when a wife knows her place."

"And you'll find it's more interesting when she doesn't," I answer, stepping ahead of him toward the next cluster of guests.

"Come," Philippe says, steering me toward a pair who radiate the kind of wealth that needs no introduction. "My parents are eager to meet their future daughter."

"Marquis Henri-Jacques de Launay," the man says, his voice clipped, as if even his name is an order. "This union will serve both our houses well."

"And I am the Marquise Élisabeth," his wife says, her green eyes sweeping over me with the precision of a jeweler examining a stone. "You are lovelier than we'd hoped."

Marquis and Marquise de Launay—all powdered curls and jeweled buttons. My mother stands just off to the side, her hand resting lightly on my father's arm, watching.

"I am glad I could surpass expectation," I reply lightly.

My mother, Marguerite's, voice slides in. "My daughter has always surpassed expectations."

"A wife," Élisabeth says, still smiling, "is a reflection of her husband's station. See that you reflect it well."

"I'll do my best to make sure Philippe's station is worth reflecting."

The Marquis' gaze snaps toward me. My father shifts beside my mother, but says nothing. Philippe chuckles, guiding me away before anyone can respond. Once we're clear of the crowd, his grip on my arm tightens.

"A word of advice, ma fiancée—you do not test my parents."

"I wasn't testing them. I was testing you."

His smile doesn't reach his eyes. "Marriage is easier when a wife knows her place."

He walks away without another word, moving toward the corner where a cluster of velvet coats call his name. Friends, I assume—though they look at me like I'm already a possession he's displaying.

I stand in the middle of the ballroom, light from the chandeliers glinting off the diamonds at my throat. Music drifts through the air, couples glide across the floor, and the scent of roses hangs heavy. It is all beautiful. It is all wrong.

My eyes sting, but I refuse to let the tears fall. Not here. Not in front of them. I lift my chin, as if posture alone could keep me from breaking.

I want to run. I want to scream. Instead, I smile at strangers who see only a well dressed daughter of a wealthy house. They do not see the girl who feels her life shrinking around her like she is walking towards the executioner's blade.

This is what I was born for. A husband I do not love. A future I cannot escape. A life that was planned for me.

And I am already mourning the woman I might have been.

Chapter Three
Liora

The crowds are gone—finally. I don't think I could take another congratulatory message from people I don't know.

I'm completely over it.

"My lady." Yvette comes up behind me. "Your father has requested that everyone prepare for dinner. Shall we change?"

I open my mouth to answer her, but Philippe speaks first. "When addressing her, you will speak to me first."

I'm too shocked to say anything at first. Yvette begins to shake next to me. I grab her hand to comfort her.

"Excuse me?" I'm sure I've misheard him. I must have.

"It's a matter of respect," he says, his voice carrying an edge to it. "When you serve my fiancée, you answer to me."

Heat rises in my chest. "You don't give orders to my household," I say evenly. I pull my hands away from Yvette's and clench my fingers in a fist, my nails biting into my skin.

His lips curve faintly, like this is some kind of game he's already won. "Not yet."

I don't respond to him—because if I do, I'll say something I can't take back.

"Yes, Yvette," I say to her instead. "Let us get ready for dinner."

I have to make nice with Philippe. If I'm going to survive this engagement, I can't make an enemy out of him before the ink is dry on the marriage contract.

I smooth my skirts, offer him a polite smile, and lean in just enough to brush a kiss against his cheek.

"I'll meet you at the table," I murmur, keeping my tone light.

I go upstairs and Yvette follows me, her quick steps muffled by the runner.

"You'll want to watch your tongue tonight," she says, not unkindly. "If you let your sarcasm run wild, you'll be serving yourself a lifetime of misery."

I nod at her. I think I did enough talking for all of us at the engagement. I can tell Yvette is worried. I've always been quick to speak and slower to think about things all the way through.

She laces me into a fresh gown for dinner, a softer blue silk that feels wonderful after being in the other dress. By the time we descend the stairs, Philippe is waiting at the foot, polished as marble, his hand resting on the banister like he's posing for a portrait.

He straightens when he sees me, bowing lightly before offering his arm. This time, his smile doesn't feel rehearsed.

"You speak too quickly sometimes," he says as we walk toward the dining hall, his tone even but not unkind. "I think that's why people whisper."

I arch a brow. "You mean my sarcasm."

He almost smiles. "If you like."

I take a breath. Normally, I'd bite back. But something in his expression—a flicker of genuine curiosity, maybe—makes me try honesty instead. "It's not just... inappropriate behavior. It's how I survive. If I don't make light of things, I feel them too deeply. If I let myself feel all of it—the politics, the expectations, the endless performance—it would crush me."

He studies me for a moment, and to my surprise, he nods. "That, I can understand. You think wit is armor."

"Do you disapprove?" I ask, quieter now.

His jaw works, but he doesn't look away. "No. I only fear what my father fears—that the world is not kind to women who wield their voices too freely. He thinks a wife should listen before she speaks. I…" He exhales.

That almost makes me laugh, and for a second, the weight on my chest loosens. "You have no idea."

His mouth twitches, almost a real grin this time. "Perhaps I will learn."

We pause outside the doors to the dining hall, voices and clinking glasses echoing from within. For a moment, it almost feels like something real could exist between us. But then he adjusts his sleeve, expression smoothing back into practiced calm.

"Come," he says, offering his arm again. "Let us play our parts."

Philippe pulls out my chair before taking his own. Henri-Jacques barely glances at me, already deep in discussion with my father.

Before me, a pheasant breast glazed in wine sauce sits untouched, its aroma rich but cloying. Beside it, a neat pile of buttered asparagus and a sugared strawberry tart I can't bring myself to taste.

"…the king's attention is a fickle thing," the Marquis is saying. "But a marriage like this—yes, this will remind the court that the Launay name still commands respect."

Marguerite, elegant even in silence, smiles thinly and turns her wineglass in her hand. "Respect is earned, Marquis, not purchased."

Élisabeth's green eyes flash, her smile equally thin. "Yet wealth and alliances have always been the surest coin in Paris. My son and your daughter are a perfect match—for beauty, for station. I imagine no one will dispute that."

Heat pricks my skin, but I force my expression to be smooth. I lift my fork, more for something to do with my hands than to eat.

Philippe clears his throat. "My fiancée is more than beauty, Mother. She has wit. Sharp wit."

Henri-Jacques waves a hand, dismissive. "Wit is wasted in a wife. Better to save her tongue for prayers and polite conversation."

The table stills. My father gives me a warning look, the kind that says *hold it in*. My mother presses her lips into a practiced smile.

I swallow hard and focus on my plate. A cage with golden hinges is still a cage.

Élisabeth dabs delicately at her mouth with a napkin. "Speaking of tongues—let us move to the matter of the wedding. The sooner it is done, the sooner Paris will see what strength looks like when two great houses unite."

Henri-Jacques nods. "By week's end, I think. Swift action speaks louder than waiting on ceremony."

The knife stills in my hand. I glance at Philippe, certain I must have misheard. But he doesn't look surprised.

Marguerite sets her glass down too sharply, the crystal ringing. "Impossible. A marriage of this scale requires the king's acknowledgment. The banns must be read, the invitations sent, the blessing secured. Do you imagine His Majesty will come running simply because you wish it?"

Henri-Jacques's jaw tightens. "The king respects efficiency."

My father clears his throat. "The king respects tradition. A month, at least, for the banns and the preparations. Anything less would be an insult to him—and to my daughter."

The word *month* spins in my head, loosening the breath in my chest. A month is still a noose, but at least it isn't tightened overnight.

Henri-Jacques leans back, clearly irritated but unwilling to press further. Élisabeth smiles again, smooth and false. "A month it is. But not a day more."

I lower my gaze to my plate, willing my hands to stop shaking. A month. Four weeks of freedom I don't deserve to cling to—but I will.

At last, Father rises. Henri-Jacques follows, both men exchanging a look I don't miss. They excuse themselves, retreating to Father's study to speak of politics, alliances, and futures traded like coin. Philippe is invited to go with him and he jumps at the chance.

That leaves us—the women. The Marquise smooths her skirts, her smile sharp as glass. My mother sits straighter, already bracing herself for battle. And me, caught in the middle, the prize they'll decorate, parade, and bind.

Élisabeth's gaze fixes on me. "Now, my dear, let us discuss your wedding."

The study doors remain closed behind the men, the low rumble of their voices muted by thick oak. Here, the battlefield is no less vicious.

Élisabeth spreads her fan across the table like a general unrolling a map. "The ceremony must be at Saint-Sulpice. Anything less would appear provincial. The Duchesne estate cannot contain the spectacle Paris demands."

My mother inclines her head. "Saint-Sulpice is... adequate. But the reception will be here. This house was built for grandeur, and grandeur it will show."

Élisabeth hums, unimpressed. "Very well. Then it must be gilded with roses. White and red, enough to perfume the entire arrondissement. Versailles will expect nothing less."

"White roses," Marguerite corrects softly. "Purity, dignity, restraint."

I say nothing. Neither of them look at me.

"The gown," Élisabeth continues, fanning herself. "Pearl embroidery, naturally. A train long enough to sweep the cathedral floor. And a diamond tiara, of course."

Marguerite's lips twitch. "Gold thread. Lyon silk. A duchess's coronet. Pearls alone are too simple."

I press my hands into my lap beneath the tablecloth. The words swirl around me like smoke. Dresses. Jewels. Roses. None of it sounds like my life. None of it feels like me.

"Guests must be selected carefully," Élisabeth adds. "The Montmorencys, certainly. The Noailles. And perhaps a discreet invitation to Versailles itself."

"Discreet?" Marguerite's voice sharpens. "We announce it boldly. Let Paris know that the Duchesne name still commands the highest respect."

Their voices grow tighter, circling each other like duelists. I sit still, a doll propped between them, my silence the one thing neither notices nor minds.

They are planning a celebration. To me, it sounds like a funeral.

At last, both women turn to me. "What would you like, ma chère?" Élisabeth asks, her smile dripping with expectation.

"Not roses. Not pearls. No powdered wigs or lace to choke on." My voice is more clipped than I intend it to be. "If it were mine to decide, the hall would be draped in black velvet and lit with a thousand flames. Music that shakes the walls. Wine that never runs dry. A crown of iron, not gold. A night no one could forget—and no one could control."

The stunned silence after is louder than any orchestra.

I lower my gaze, forcing a small smile. "But of course, tradition is tradition. Roses will do."

They take my answer as permission and fall right back into chatter. Roses. Lilies. Gold-threaded gowns. Pearls stitched into my hair so I can glitter like some prized ornament.

On the surface, I nod. Inside, I'm screaming and raging.

Every suggestion sounds like another nail in a coffin I didn't build. They speak of pastel silks, of ivory lace, of lightness and purity—when there is nothing light or pure about binding two strangers together for power. They talk as though beauty is obedience, as though a painted face and a docile smile will make me a good wife.

My mother murmurs approval when Élisabeth suggests a dove release. The Marquise claps her hands at the thought of Versailles envying the spectacle. And me? I sit, I listen, I sip wine.

But in my mind, I see black banners. Smoke curling through chandeliers. Not a wedding—an execution dressed in silk.

The doors to the study open. Philippe bursts out, his grin too wide, his cheeks flushed with triumph. He looks like a man who has just won the world.

"Our future begins," he declares, striding toward me. Before I can move, his hand catches mine, and his lips brush my cheek. Our family applaud, some even laugh with delight at the display.

Everyone smiles. Everyone but me.

Because I am not ready. Not for him. Not for this.

Chapter Four
Liora

A month to the day. Marquise Élisabeth wasn't kidding. Not a day later.

Yvette and my mother are already fussing over my hair and makeup when Élisabeth de Launay sweeps in like a winter draft.

"Oh dear," she says, her eyes scanning me like I'm a flawed gemstone. "We'll need to adjust that color. Too much rose in the cheeks. Makes her look unseemingly."

My mother stiffens but says nothing. Yvette quietly sets down the blush brush.

"It's the natural flush of youth," she says softly, smoothing a hand over my shoulder.

Élisabeth hums. "Youth is charming. But this isn't a debutante ball. A duchess must radiate composure. Not sentiment."

She moves closer, her gloved hand tilting my chin to inspect the angle. "Hair tighter. No wisps. Men find messiness endearing, but we're not dressing for their amusement. We're dressing for dominance."

Yvette exchanges a glance with my mother, who reluctantly nods.

"Yes, Madame," Yvette says, beginning to unpin the curls she'd so carefully arranged.

I sit still, staring at myself in the mirror as they remake me. Hair pulled back like I'm being reeled in. Skin powdered pale. Lips reddened to look like I bleed elegance.

"I look like someone else," I say quietly.

My mother meets my gaze in the glass. Her expression softens just enough to hurt. "You look like the wife of a future duke."

"No," Élisabeth corrects smoothly. "She looks like a Launay. As she should."

I don't answer. If I open my mouth, I might scream. Or sob. Or say something that turns this room into a battlefield.

"Come," Élisabeth says. "We must go. The ceremony is starting soon."

Again, I have no opinion. It never matters. I just go with it.

The ride to the church feels like an eternity. People stare and wave like I'm royalty. The streets are lined with well wishers.

I sink into the seat more, not wanting to be seen.

"We're here," Élisabeth says, gleefully clapping her hands.

I follow my mother and soon to be mother-in-law out of the carriage. We lift our skirts to remain dust free.

Saint-Sulpice rises before us—massive, austere, and unfinished in its crown but no less imposing.

White rose petals litter the stone steps, and attendants in pale gloves sweep them constantly to make room for more. The bells begin to toll. My mother says something to Élisabeth beside her, but I don't hear it. All I hear is the silence that waits inside those doors.

My life will begin and end at the same time. Only to be followed by children and a family.

It's so overwhelming I feel like I'm going to hyperventilate right here.

I'm hurried into a room just as ornate as the rest of the place, and the door shuts behind me, muffling the sounds of the world outside.

For a moment, there's nothing. Just hushed voices running around. The lace hem of my gown trailing over polished stone. My own footsteps echo like a heartbeat in a tomb.

I walk to the mirror. The woman staring back isn't me.

Her hair is sculpted high, stiff with pearls and powder. Her gown—a cathedral of silk and stitching—gleams like it belongs to a statue, not a living, breathing person. Her face is painted into perfection, but the eyes...

The pain in the eyes is all mine.

I reach for the glass like I could touch her, like I could beg her to trade places. She doesn't move. Doesn't blink.

She looks like a bride. I feel like a corpse.

A sound tears out of my throat—half sob, half gasp—and I stumble backward, knocking a silver tray off the dressing table. Perfume bottles crash to the floor, glass shattering, rosewater blooming like blood on the marble.

I clutch the edge of the table, fingers white.

I wanted to be strong.

But I can't breathe.

This isn't my life. This isn't my choice. This isn't *me*.

I was supposed to fall in love. To have a partner, not someone over me, not someone telling me to watch my tone. I was supposed to matter more than dowries and titles and well practiced smiles.

Instead, I'm here. Painted, packaged, and poised to be handed off like a letter of credit.

And no one—not my father, not Philippe, not even my mother—has asked if I want this.

Tears blur my reflection. My chest heaves. I walk back and press both hands to the mirror, my forehead resting against cool glass, hoping it might calm the fire underneath my skin.

I don't want to go out there.

I don't want to become someone I don't recognize.

But I will.

Because the doors will open. Because I've been taught to smile. Because I'm not supposed to run.

Even when everything inside me already has.

"It is time, my dear," my mother says, while opening the door.

For a second, her mask slips. She takes a long look at me. I'm still her daughter, but wrapped in something that isn't me.

She doesn't cry. Or protest. I know she did everything for me that she could. She tried to stop this. The crown desires the union. They get the union.

"You look beautiful," she says, voice full of pain. This is hurting her almost as much as it hurts me.

I muster a nod and smooth my hands down my dress. Holding my head up high, I walk out of the room and to the massive double doors ahead of me.

My father stands near the chapel doors, hands clasped behind his back, speaking with the priest in hushed tones. Across the room, three unfamiliar women stand in a perfect triangle of lace and expectation.

My ladies-in-waiting, I assume. Chosen not for loyalty, but for lineage.

They don't speak when I enter. They don't need to.

Their eyes sweep over me in unison—not with admiration, but calculation. One tilts her head, lips curving in a smile that doesn't reach her eyes. Another murmurs something to the third behind a gloved hand. They laugh.

I meet their eyes, just long enough for one to blink and look away.

My mother smooths the back of my gown, her fingers gentle where theirs would not be. "Hold your chin high," she whispers. "They can't touch what they can't reach."

My father offers his arm without a word, his eyes fixed straight ahead. We take the first step together, and then he leans in just enough for me to hear.

"You're doing the right thing," he murmurs. "Hold your head high. All of Paris is watching."

I don't answer. I can't. My throat is too tight. Ahead, Philippe waits beneath the altar's gilded arch.

He wears a pale ivory coat embroidered with gold thread, the cuffs stiff with lace, a jeweled cravat pinned at his throat like a brooch on a mannequin. His powdered wig is flawless—each curl sculpted into place, dusted with a hint of lavender to match the ribbons at his sleeves. His shoes gleam with polished gold buckles, heels clicking softly as he shifts from side to side.

He looks like a prince from a painting.

I reach the altar, my hand trembling as I slide it into his. His fingers curl around mine automatically—firm, rehearsed, and just a little too tight. He doesn't look at me. Just nods to the priest like a man shaking hands before closing a deal.

The priest's voice rises, solemn and rehearsed. "We are gathered here in sacred union, to bind two souls in the eyes of God, the crown, and the law."

Philippe's hand finds mine again, firm and possessive. I don't look at him. I can't. My eyes fix on a stained glass window above the altar—red and gold shards catching sunlight like fire. I imagine stepping through it. Shattering it. Anything but standing still.

Beside me, Philippe shifts slightly, as if impatient for the performance to end.

The priest continues. "Marriage is not only a joining of hearts, but of houses, of names, of legacy—"

Legacy. That's all I've ever been. A continuation. A transaction.

I don't listen. Not really. It's just a bunch of words about being faithful, which I know he won't be.

"Repeat after me," the priest says to Phillipe.

Philippe tilts his chin slightly upward, like he's accepting applause before it even starts.

"I, Philippe François de Launay," the priest intones.

"I, Philippe François de Launay," Philippe repeats. He glances briefly at the crowd—as if he wants to make sure they heard him.

"Take you, Liora Duchesne, to be my lawfully wedded wife."

"Take you, Liora Duchesne, to be my lawfully wedded wife," he says, lips curving faintly. Like he's tasting victory.

I hear the words. I do. But they land somewhere far away.

"Before God, the crown, and our families," the priest continues.

Philippe shifts slightly, straightening his shoulders with pride. "Before God, the crown, and our families," he echoes, louder this time. More for them than for me.

I focus on the stained glass above the altar. A saint holding a sword. I count the red panes in his robe. Anything but listening.

The priest turns to me. It's my turn for the vows.

"Mademoiselle Liora Duchesne, daughter of House Duchesne," he says, his voice echoing beneath the vaulted stone, "repeat after me."

My heart speeds up, rattling in my chest like a drum. I hate this with all of my being.

"I, Liora Duchesne, take you, Philippe François de Launay, to be my lawfully wedded husband. I vow to stand beside you in faith and duty, to honor our union before God, the crown, and our families, and to uphold the name and legacy entrusted to me. I pledge my loyalty, my obedience, and my household, to serve with grace, to walk in virtue, and to bind my life to yours, now and forever."

I repeat every word the priest says, my voice holds until the final line. That one catches. I stutter. Just once.

Philippe's gaze snaps to mine, and his fingers tighten. A warning dressed as a gesture of support. He laughs awkwardly and clears his throat.

I start the last line. "and to bind my life to yours, now and—"

The doors burst open. Wood slams against stone with a sound like thunder. Gasps ripple through the crowd, followed by a scream from Élisabeth in the front row.

I see him. A man.

He strides into the church like he's got the power of God himself. He's tall, dark, and everything no one here would dare touch. His coat is black velvet with silver embroidery trailing the seams like veins. His boots strike the stone with purpose, not ceremony. His dark hair is a little wild, just long enough to curl past his jaw.

And god—he's beautiful.

Not the same as others here with their powdered wigs and desire to be in court. Not like Philippe with his curled wig and glassy smile. This man is rough edges and burning blood.

His eyes lock on mine and everything stops. His body stills. He lifts his left sleeve.

I don't know why.

At first, I think he's reaching for a weapon. But then I see it—something glowing faintly beneath his skin. A scar? Or a burn?

My stomach twists.

He looks down. Not at my face, but lower. At my collarbone.

The pain is immediate. Violent. Wrong. Like a hot iron driven through my chest, straight into the bone. I can't scream fast enough.

It tears through me like parchment curling black at the edges, like ink turned to blood.

My knees collapse beneath me. My hand claws at the neckline of my gown, desperate to tear the heat away, but there's nothing—no flame, no brand, just searing agony that feels holy and damned all at once.

Is this divine punishment? Did I blaspheme? Or has hell itself reached for me in front of God and crown?

Philippe drops to his knees beside me.

"Liora," he says, grabbing my arm. "Liora, look at me." His voice cracks on the second call, and still—I can't answer. I can barely see him through the blur of pain.

He shakes me once, gentle but desperate. "What's happening? Speak to me!"

Philippe rises, voice sharp and frantic. "You! Get away from her! We had a deal!"

Suddenly I'm not on the stone floor anymore. I'm in someone's arms—his arms. He holds me like I'm not a girl collapsing in front of a church full of strangers, but something precious. Like I've always been meant to fit right there.

I blink up at him, breathless, stunned.

He's close now. Closer than anyone has ever dared be.

His eyes—gold threaded with flame—look straight into me, past the pain, past the fear, past the ceremony.

"I'm Evander."

The air hums.

"You've been mine since the first breath your soul ever took." His mouth finds the corner of mine—not a kiss. A promise. "And I swear it now, my dove—I'll burn kingdoms, gods, and bloodlines before I let you go."

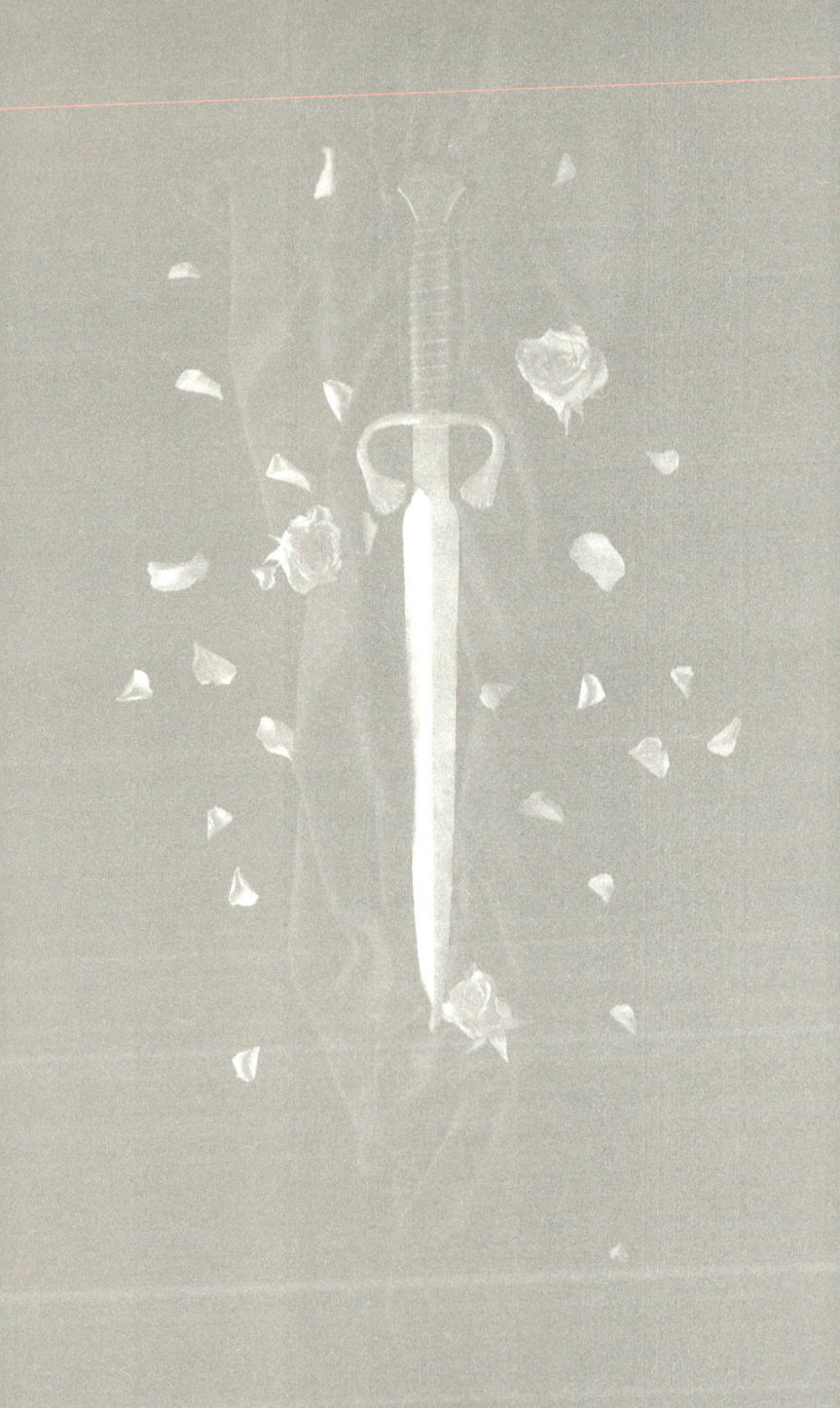

Chapter Five
Evander

I arrive at the church. Saint-Sulpice I believe it's called. There is clearly a celebration here today.

I've been spending most of my time in Hell catching up on contracts. Paperwork is the worst. One day I hope there's a group to handle it. I can just hand it to them and walk my ass away. But for now, it's just me.

I felt this weird pull or call. That's why I'm here. I've never experienced it before. This longing and want.

It feels meant to be in a way that I can't explain. I always do easy. Sleep with a mortal, leave. Done.

I don't want that anymore.

Walking up to the front, I see the banner. Philippe and Liora.

Liora. There's that name again. The one that I can't seem to get out of my head for the life of me.

I hear music and know whatever is going on, is probably important. I just follow the pull to the massive wooden doors.

I lean close and listen to Philippe say his vows. De Lauray. *Well fuck me!* I made a deal with them. Is it already up?

No. I know what that feels like. This isn't it. It's so much more.

I throw the wooden doors open and see her.

Draped in gold-threaded silk, she stands beneath vaulted stone like some divine offering—flawless, untouched, adorned. Every inch of her sculpted by someone else's vision of perfection.

It's not her.

Not the woman my blood burns for. Not the soul that calls mine like thunder.

It's a costume.

I look at my arm and see the sign I've only yearned for. The mark of Duvain. It's shifting under my skin, blooming into my being.

I look up at Liora and she drops to the ground, writhing in pain.

Philippe drops to his knees beside her.

"Liora," he says, clutching her arm like it'll bring her back. "Liora, look at me." His voice cracks. She doesn't respond. Can't. Her face twists in pain so deep it looks like it's devouring her from the inside.

He shakes her, gently—but it's desperation, not tenderness. "What's happening? Speak to me!"

She doesn't.

Because she's not his to save.

Philippe rises, spinning toward me like a man losing everything he never truly earned. "You!" he shouts, voice ragged. "Get away from her! We had a deal!"

I completely ignore him and walk towards her. She is in pain. My heart feels like it's breaking in two, tearing at the edges. I need to fix it, she cannot be in pain, not while I still draw breath.

I pick her up in my arms and rock her relevantly. She doesn't fight it. She melts into me like she's always belonged there.

She blinks up at me, dazed with pain still shadowing her eyes. But underneath it is recognition. The bond humming to life between us.

I lower my head until I'm close—closer than anyone has ever dared be.

Her face is drawn, pale, lips parted in shock.

Gods, she's real.

I look straight into her—past the silk, the pain, the cage they wrapped her in.

"I'm Evander."

The air tightens. The mark on my arm burns hot.

"You've been mine since the first breath your soul ever took."

I press my mouth to the corner of hers—not a kiss. A claim. A vow carved into fate.

"And I swear it now, dove—I'll burn kingdoms, gods, and bloodlines before I let you go."

She looks at me and smiles. I can't help it. I smile back.

"You get off of my bride," Philippe says.

"Nope. She's mine. Remember our deal, De Launay?" I tisk. "See you lost something desirable. It just so happens to be your bride."

"She would never choose you," he sneers.

I see her struggling to get up and I help her.

"You mean I have a choice?" She asks in hushed tones.

"You do," I confirm.

I can see it in her eyes—the first flicker of rebellion. The moment her mind shifts from obedience to possibility.

But before she can speak again, cold footsteps echo across the marble.

"Of course she has a choice," Lady de Launay cuts in, voice polished sharp. "And she's made it. Haven't you, dear?"

She doesn't wait for an answer. Her eyes slide to me with disdain.

"Leave now, whoever you are. You've embarrassed yourself enough."

"He's nothing," De Launay growls. "No name, no seal, no claim. This union is protected by the crown—"

I step forward, still holding Liora in my arms.

"Protected by lies," I say, low and calm. "She was never yours to give."

Philippe surges forward with a snarl, drawing a blade that flashes in the sunlight. "Put her down!"

I don't.

He swings. I catch his wrist. The blade clatters to the floor, and I shove him back without effort. He stumbles. Someone gasps.

"Try again," I tell him, voice dark. "See how far your father's dowry gets you."

Lady de Launay steps forward, fury tightening her face. "You're a curse," she spits. "A disruption."

I look at her and I smile.

"No. I'm so much more than that." My eyes burn red. "I'm her fate."

"I choose Evander," Liora announces. Her voice is raspy. She had to muster up the power to speak. The bond is still making her weak.

Her parents are still seated. They don't get involved. If anything else, the slight look of relief on their faces shocks me. They truly just want what's best for their daughter. I put her in this mess with the deal.

"You don't mean that," Philippe starts. He never gets to finish. She won't let him.

The look on his face says it all. Philippe François de Launay is not used to being denied. This is the man who gets whatever he wants, never has to beg, and no woman would dare turn him down.

"I do. He gave me a choice. You did not. You made a *deal*. Was it for me? For power?" She crosses her arms over her chest.

He starts to panic. He's called out. Everyone here knows that he is a weak mortal.

"Well—I—See I— It was my father's idea!" Philippe stammers, pointing to the Marquis like a child caught stealing bread.

A hush ripples through the church. There are murmurs and some gasps here and there.

I was not expecting that. Throwing his father into the mix. Not someone who can take accountability for anything. He was the one who initiated the deal to begin with.

The Marquise de Launay's fan snaps closed with a crack. Her eyes cut to her son—fury, shame, and disbelief all warring behind a mask of powder and pearls.

The Marquis, stiff and scarlet, doesn't speak. Doesn't move. His nostrils flare, his hands clench at his sides.

Philippe's finger still hangs in the air. No one defends him.

"No backbone runs in the family," I say, smirking at him. "What do you say, Dove? Want to take a chance?"

I watch as the storm of emotions run behind her eyes—pain, defiance, fear, something like hope. She's deciding what she wants. I don't think she's ever truly believed she could.

"Yes," she says, power exuding from her being. "I choose you. I am ready to take a chance—for me."

I hold my hand out to her and she slides hers in mine. I feel flames scorching up my arm. *Yeah this is what I've always wanted.*

"No!" Philippe shouts. He takes Liora's arm and pulls her to his body, holding her close. He wraps her tight and pulls her behind him. "She is *mine*. We had a *deal*. We signed in *blood*."

I see it the moment it happens. Her eyes go from amber to red, swirling in the depths of her pupils. I know this is going to be interesting.

I lean back and smirk, crossing my arms.

"What are you smiling at?!" Philippe demands.

"Oh you'll see," I say, cryptically on purpose. He doesn't need me to tell him. He's about to experience the wrath of my soulmate.

"Don't you dare *touch* me!" She shoves him away with enough force to knock him off balance. He trips on his heels and falls embarrassingly to the floor.

"I am not yours," she spits at him. "I was *never* yours!"

Her voice cracks as she starts tearing at the gown—jewels falling to the floor. She pulls the dress off, leaving her in just a corset and those odd wide pants the women are forced to wear.

Women in the pews gasp and pretend to faint. Some may not be faking it. I let out a boisterous laugh as she pulls her curls down.

"I am done playing your bride." She's leaning over Philippe now in nothing but her undergarments. "I'd rather walk barefoot in Hell than stay bound to you."

I let out a boisterous laugh as she pulls her curls down, shaking them loose like she's shedding her skin.

"Liora!" The priest snaps from beside us, already halfway to pull Liora away from prying eyes. "Compose yourself!"

She doesn't. She turns.

And punches him right in the nose.

Then the carpet ignites.

Blue flames crawl outward from her bare feet like they've been waiting centuries for this cue. The aisle becomes a burning path, smoke curling toward the vaulted ceiling.

She looks at me and walks over. Her hand grabs mine and she gives me a soft smile. One that is only for me now. "I'm ready when you are."

And just like that—she becomes everything they never let her be.

Chapter Six
Liora

He doesn't waste another second before pulling me away. I run behind him. We get out of the doors and he wraps his coat around me.

It's at that moment that I realized I'm in nothing but my undergarments.

My parents walk up to us.

"I don't want to hear it," I say, my voice tight. I know how I must sound. Like I'm whining and defiant. I never act this way. Unless it's important.

My mother's face immediately softens. Her eyes are shadowed with grief, but even more so, love. She steps closer to us, lifting her hand to touch my cheek. I can feel her tremble and grab her hand, holding it tight.

"We're not here to tell you no," my mother says, clinging to hope and holding back tears.

My father stands beside her. No disappointment in his eyes. Just questions.

"We love you and always want what's best," my father adds. He turns his attention to my... Evander? "This deal you spoke about..."

Evander looks wary for a second before wiping his face to a neutral stance.

"Yes?" Evander asks.

My mother's brow furrows. She looks as if she is caught between heartbreak and confusion.

"Is it true?" I can tell he's hoping Evander will say no, but he knows that it's no use. He knows what we all do. It's a fact.

My mother's lips part, but no words come out. She doesn't want to admit that her and my father almost married me off to a madman.

"It is," Evander confirms.

"That's all I needed to know," my father says. He walks back into the church, marching up to Philippe and his father, and without warning, punches him right in the face.

Evander is laughing and I'm in awe. Marquise is babying her husband and son, shooting glares in our direction.

"That is for my daughter!" My father shouts. "Ladies and gentleman, I apologize for having all you gather for this. My daughter will never marry such a disgrace. If I were you, I would shun the De Laurays. The king will surely do the same."

He walks away and the Marquise grabs his arm. "No! Henri, no! You will ruin our name."

"Firstly, you do not have the authority to address me as such," he scoffs, before continuing. "Secondly, your husband and son have done a fine job of ruining it themselves." He shakes her arm off as she collapses to the floor with none of the grace she had held so dear.

I hug my parents. I love them dearly. I don't know what's going to happen next. But there's something in the air that tells me I may not see them for quite some time. When I turn my tear filled gaze back to Evander, it's almost like he reads my mind.

"Don't worry, Dove." He pulls me close, rubbing my back lovingly. "You will never lose them. I won't take them from you. We can visit whenever you desire."

I really let myself see him—the man I do not know, but know completely. The man I chose to turn my world upside down.

His hair is nearly black, a stark contrast to the powdered and polished world I was raised in. His shoulders are broad, his skin smooth—regal and timeless. Like he's stepped out of another world somehow untouched by age. He must age...but if he does, he hides it well.

His eyes—amber threaded with red—flicker like embers submerged in water.

He is magnificent. The most devastatingly beautiful man I've ever seen.

We run towards the door, and throw one last look over my shoulder. My parents give me a teary smile. People are filing out of the church, whispering to each other behind their fans. Philippe has dropped to his knees, hand buried in his hands living with the shame he deserves.

Hopefully this is the last time I'll ever see him.

Evander glances around the courtyard quickly before pulling me behind a large planter bursting with flowers.

"I'm going to show you something," he says.

I don't respond—I'm not sure I can even if I tried. He is already a walking mystery, and I'm hungry for each and every detail he's willing to give me.

He brushes my hair back, his fingertips trace around my cheek and go down to my chin. The sun is setting in the background and it feels like I'm in a dream, not reality.

Evander: *Can you hear me?*

"What—" I break off. I heard it. I know I did. But I studied his lips and they never moved. Not once.

Evander: *I know you can, Dove.*

Liora: *Did you just...communicate with me? Without speaking?*

Evander: *I did. Soulmates. We communicate this way.*

"Soulmate?" I ask aloud. That word—it knocks something loose in me. He needs to explain. I have no idea what that is. Everything feels out of my control. My heart rate ticks up, my chest is heavy. But when I meet his eyes, I start to calm.

He studies me, holding my attention hostage, as if he knows that I need him to ground me. "A soulmate is the lifeblood of a demon. The only thing that matters to us. It's the deepest bond that exists. The purest form of love in the universe."

But I'm stuck on one word. *Demon.*

Is he saying he is a demon? Am I a demon? How many demons are there? Are they as the church describes? I cannot imagine this walking work of art in front of me as an evil entity.

"Yes, I am a demon," he says and smiles—almost like he expected the question. "You are not. You are a mate of one. There are many of us," he chuckles.

"Right," I say, sighing. I rub my aching temples. "You can hear my thoughts."

He laughs again and the sound pierces me. It splits something open in my chest that has been locked away my entire life.

My heart stumbles.

I've never heard anything like it. Almost as if I took a gulp of hot tea on a cold, winter night. It's a breath of fresh air. Not stiff or awkward.

Without thinking—without a single conscious thought—I lean in.

My lips find his. Awkward at first. I've never done this before. My mouth brushes his more than kisses him. I start to panic.

He doesn't laugh at me. He tips my face up with his finger just enough for me to see his eyes swirling red.

"Slow," he murmurs. "Like this."

He leans in, brushing his mouth over mine again. It's just a ghost of a touch. "It's not a race, Dove. Just let yourself feel it."

I mimic his every movement, pressing into him more fully this time. He exhales into my mouth. His muscles are tense. Like he's restraining himself from pushing me too far out of my comfort zone. His thumb brushes over my cheek again, encouraging me to continue.

"That's it," he whispers. "Let yourself want it."

My hands press against his chest, and I can feel the heat of him through his shirt. He's solid and steady on his feet while I feel like a feather could knock me over. Everything in me is trembling. I want more.

His mouth parts slightly, and our lips move again. They dance in harmony as he deepens the kiss even more. His thumb brushes over my ear lobe and I swear I melt into him.

"You're doing perfect," he says against my lips. He knows all the right words. He can feel that I was doubting myself and in one moment, he alleviates all the fears I have.

I always thought a woman was to be lesser than, but he makes me feel like his queen. Though here, there is no court or titles.

Just him and me. Together as one. For eternity as he claims.

And this kiss that feels like the start of something I can't undo.

I breathe him in—he smells like heat and smoke and something richer underneath. His lips are warm, sure. And when my fingers slide up to the back of his neck, he groans—low and quiet, like he's been holding it in for years.

The sound does something to me.

My knees go weak. Heat pools low in my stomach.

I press closer.

His hand slides to my waist, careful, restrained. But he doesn't pull me in—I move there myself.

And when I do, he lets out another one of those groans, this one a little more ragged.

It's my first kiss. But it doesn't feel that way. It feels like I've done this a thousand times. In dreams. In lifetimes I don't remember. Like my soul has always known the shape of his mouth.

When I finally pull back, I'm breathless.

His eyes are still closed. His chest rising and falling like he just fought a battle.

When he opens them, they're glowing. I laugh. I can't help it. My fingers are still tangled in his hair. My mouth still tingles.

"You kissed me," I whisper.

"No, Dove," he murmurs, leaning in to brush his lips against mine again, slower this time, more possessive. "You kissed me first. I'll never forget it."

"I've never kissed anyone before," I admit.

"I know," he says. "But I swear, you just ruined me for anyone else. But we're not done yet. I have another thing to show you."

He looks around the courtyard, checking it's empty before waving a hand through the air. A strange cloud appears—grey fading to black. Bone white branches twist around the edges, and the air seems to be sucked inward, spinning slowly.

"What is that?" I ask, breath caught in my throat. I want to reach out and touch it. I cast a hesitant look at Evander, there's an instinct inside of me that knows he'd never let anything bad happen to me. He doesn't stop me, so I do it. The air around it stirs, brushing against my finger tips.

"The sun is setting," he says, eyes shining bright. "How about we have some fun?"

He holds out his hand, letting me make the decision. I grab it and he pulls me through. My scream leads us to the darkness. In what feels like a second, we pop out.

Right on some freezing ground.

The cold stings as the wind whips my skin. We're surrounded by white—soft, deep, and endless. A blizzard rages around us. We're high up on a mountain.

"Where are we?" I spin around slowly in complete awe. It's like nothing I've ever seen before. The beauty here is unmatched.

"We're in the Swiss Alps," he replies, as if it's the most casual thing in the entire world. "Come. I have a house up here."

But this isn't just a house.

It's an estate, at least twice the size of my parents', cut into the mountainside like a palace of stone and glass, lit from within like it's alive.

What in the world have I gotten myself into?

"This is mine. I built it for no one...until now," he says.

We walk inside, warmth wrapping around me instantly. A fire crackles in the hearth.

"Theron," Evander mutters under his breath.

"Theron?" I arch a brow.

"My brother," he says with a half-smile. "You'll meet him and his soulmate soon."

"Fortune favors the bold," I say, deadpan.

Evander actually chokes—coughs once, then laughs like I sucker punched him with it.

I lift a hand. "I know. I know. But I've spent the last month with Philippe. Some things get in."

"He infected you with Virgil?"

"Only the worst parts." I grin. "If I start quoting Ovid, kill me now." We just met, but we already have the foundation of a relationship, we have an instant connection.

His eyes are still amused, but there's something else under it now. Curious. Watching me like I'm an equation he just discovered is unsolvable.

"You don't talk like someone newly pulled from a church," he says, tone mild.

"That's because you didn't see the wedding menu."

He laughs again. We settle into the silence like it was waiting for us. I don't know how long we sit there, close but not quite touching. There's wine—dark, heady—and firelight, flickering like it's got secrets. The kind of night you don't rush.

"So," he says after a while, swirling his glass like he's trying to read the future in it. "Liora Duchesne. Who were you before the mark?"

I study the flames. "A pawn in a silk dress. A nobleman's daughter, a merchant's price tag. Philippe called me a prize."

He makes a sound low in his throat. "And now?"

I look at him. Direct. "Now I get to choose."

He nods, like that answer matters more than I know.

"And you?" I ask. "You were born to this. You've had your whole life before me. What do you even ask someone like me?"

He leans back, arm draped over the back of the couch. Casual. But his eyes are anything but. "I ask what you loved before you were told not to."

That gets me.

I take a sip, slower this time. "Books. The wrong ones. Mythology, philosophy. My father said too much thinking made a woman bitter."

"He was half right," Evander murmurs.

I raise an eyebrow.

"Thinking makes a woman dangerous."

The tension tightens—just a notch. But I feel it. We both do.

"I liked stargazing," I admit. "Not because it was romantic—because it was infinite. No one could control it."

He studies me like I'm something ancient and rare. Like he's trying to see the constellations inside me.

"Tell me something no one else knows."

I hesitate. "I was going to run. This morning. Before the wedding. I'd packed my things. I had a carriage waiting."

"What stopped you?"

"You." I exhale. "Apparently. Also my family. I couldn't do that to them."

His gaze darkens, but not with regret. With understanding.

"I didn't want a marriage," I say. "I wanted peace. Freedom."

"And now?"

I hold his eyes. "I don't know yet. But I'm here. That's something."

The air hums. He shifts slightly, just enough for our knees to brush.

"You're not what I expected either," I whisper.

"Let me guess. More horns?"

"Less... human. Less funny."

He leans in. "Don't tell anyone. I've got a reputation to ruin."

Time stretches. He watches my mouth like it's a question he's dying to answer.

I don't move. We're on the edge of something.

"Ask me anything," I say. "If we're doing this—whatever *this* is—we should at least start with honesty."

He nods slowly. "What scares you?"

I blink. I expected flirtation. Not that. After just a moment to compose myself, I answer. "Not being believed. Not being seen. Becoming invisible even when I'm screaming."

Something shifts in his face. Like I hit a nerve he didn't expect.

"You?" I ask.

He hesitates. "That I'll ruin it. That I'll hurt what I want to protect."

There's silence. Heavy. Not awkward—intimate.

I set my glass down.

He does the same and he watches me for a long beat.

I tilt my head. "You know everything about my family. But what about yours? You said you have a brother... what about your parents?"

His expression shifts—just enough to make me sit up straighter.

"Cassian and Serenya Duvain," he says quietly. "They never bowed. Not to the High Court. Not to the old powers. Not even when the world turned against them."

"Why?"

"Because they believed in something. In structure. In law. In holding the line when everything around you craves disorder." His voice has gone low, like he's reciting something etched in bone. "They supported the formation of the Infernal Council. The first real system our kind ever had—a way to bring order to what was once just fear and territory. But when the revolution came, when the underworld splintered and demons began demanding blood over balance..." He pauses, jaw tight. "They refused to turn on what they'd helped build."

"And they were killed for it?"

He nods. "Publicly. No trial. Just a message: choose the right side, or be erased."

My skin prickles. "I don't know enough about any of this. Who even are the Council?"

Evander exhales slowly. He's processing how to explain the council. I can see his eyes moving back and forth. Almost like he is preparing me for a battle I have never experienced before and maybe never again.

"Seven seats. Each one represents a ruling dominion—contracts, punishment, temptation, conquest, shadows, decay, and judgment. Each domain keeps a piece of the system running. It's not perfect, but it's functional. The Council keeps Hell from eating itself alive."

"Your parents believed in that?" I move closer to him, leaning into his body. I'm completely engulfed in his words. No other man has ever kept my attention. Philippe certainly didn't in the month I knew him.

"They helped design parts of it." He glances away for a beat. "They believed demons could be more than chaos and hunger. That we could evolve."

"Let me guess. The revolution didn't?"

"The revolution wanted blood. Power without restraint. They saw the Council as betrayal. As weakness." He looks back at me. "My parents died because they chose principle over violence. Because they wouldn't perform outrage just to survive."

"What about Theron?"

"He was closer to them. He understood what they were fighting for. But when they were executed, he ran. He couldn't stay in a world that would kill our parents and pretend it was necessary. That is, until he found his soulmate."

"And you?" I whisper.

"I stayed. I adapted. I learned how to build something no one could take from me." He pauses. "I thought that was the only way to survive."

I don't speak. I just study him—the calm in his voice, the control in his posture—but something's shifting underneath.

"Can I ask another thing?" I say, quieter now. When he smiles at me, it gives me a boost of confidence. "What is Hell really like?"

He blinks. Then smiles—just a little. "It's not fire and chains, if that's what you're imagining."

"That's exactly what I'm imagining." I giggle and reposition myself on the couch, getting more comfortable.

He leans back, letting his voice settle into something almost reverent. "Hell is ancient. Older than belief. It's cities carved into obsidian cliffs, lit by moons that never rise in the same place twice. Streets that echo with music you can't hear until you've died at least once."

I blink. I wasn't expecting poetry.

"There's a place near the southern range where the sky turns violet when it rains, and the rain sings when it hits the stone. We call it the Mourning Coast. No one remembers why anymore."

"That sounds... beautiful."

"It is," he says. "It's jagged and wild and unforgiving. But it's home. For those who know how to listen, it gives back."

"Gives back how?"

"Memory. Power. Sanctuary." He glances at me. "There's a market in the City of Ashes where every stall trades in something different—secrets, dreams, voices lost in death. You can spend a decade in one alley and never come out the same."

I exhale slowly. "Why doesn't anyone talk about this?"

"Because people need monsters. It's easier to imagine Hell as punishment than to admit it's complicated. Sacred, even."

"You make it sound like magic."

"Magic is just law written in language the living don't understand." His voice drops, and it hits somewhere deep in my very soul. "Hell isn't the absence of beauty. It's the price of it."

I stare at him. I'm not afraid of him or Hell. I want to understand all of it. Every little detail of this mysterious place. "So... is everyone there? All the damned?"

He tilts his head. "All souls pass through Hell eventually. Some stay. Most don't. It's not about punishment. It's about what's left of you when everything else is stripped away."

My brow furrows. "But the stories—torture, fire, judgment..."

"Those happen," he says simply. "But only to those who earned it. The truly corrupted. The ones who enjoyed their cruelty. Most souls... they pass through. Rest. Forget. Begin again."

I blink. "That's not what I was taught."

"Mortals build stories to make sense of the dark," he says, gently. "They needed a place to fear, and so they created one. Fire. Chains. Devils with pitchforks." He smiles slightly. "They got the demons right, at least."

"You mean the 'walking the earth' part?"

"That and the deals. But only with those who already have a black heart. We don't twist anyone. We just open the door they were already standing in front of."

I look at him differently now. Not just with curiosity. With awe.

"So you've walked the living world?"

"Many times." His voice goes quiet.

I pull my legs closer to my chest, curling inward like I need to make space for everything he's just said. "This sounds more like the Greek underworld than what I was raised to fear."

He looks at me, intrigued now. "You studied mythology?"

"Obsessively." I smile. "Hades and Persephone. The judges. The rivers. Tartarus, Lethe, Elysium... I knew it was metaphor, not reality. But there was structure to it. A logic. It always felt too specific to be just imagination."

Evander nods. "It isn't real. But it's not wrong. Mortals have always sensed pieces of the truth and shaped them into myth. Some stories echo closer than others."

"So the Council—?"

"Isn't mythology," he says, calm but certain. "It's real. Seven seats, seven dominions. Together, they keep the underworld from collapsing in on itself."

I exhale, slowly. "It sounds like a dream."

"It's home," he says.

"Do you love it?" I ask.

He doesn't even hesitate. "I do."

I'm quiet for a long moment, letting everything he's told me settle in. The cities. The sky. The laws older than stories.

Then softly, almost as if I'm speaking to myself. "I think I'll love it too."

My body sinks against the armrest, suddenly aware of how long this day has been. How surreal. How much I've survived.

He sees it. Of course he does.

"Lie down," he says softly. "You can talk. I'll listen."

I do. Not all the way—just enough to rest my head against the edge of the couch, legs tucked beneath me. He doesn't move closer. He doesn't need to.

"I like this," I whisper.

"What?"

"This. Getting to know you."

He leans his head back. His voice is lower now, matching mine. "Then let's stay here a little longer. Just like this."

My eyes drift shut.

"Liora?"

"Mmm?"

"I'm glad it was me."

I don't open my eyes.

I don't have to.

I fall asleep to the sound of him breathing next to me. For once, I don't dream of anything at all.

Chapter Seven
Evander

I wake up first, with Liora wrapped in my arms. We're exactly where she fell asleep the night before.

Most think we don't need to sleep. We're demons afterall, but that couldn't be further from the truth. We still have some mortality in us. Though not as much as a human would have.

Liora rolls around and looks at me. Her eyes are still drooping from sleep.

She stretches beside me, slow and easy. The blanket slips to her waist, and the first light turns her skin to gold.

"You're awake," she says, her voice still slightly gravely. She glances at me, lips curved. She stands up looking at me.. "I've never slept with a man before."

I raise a brow, a smirk forming at my lips. "Innocent phrasing. Dangerous delivery."

"That's not what I meant." She's flushed from the top of her head to her neck as she covers her beautiful face with small, delicate hands.

"I know exactly what you meant," I say softly, pushing her hands down gently. "I'm honored either way."

"What comes next?" She asks, tilting her head slightly.

"What's next," I say, "is your choice."

She crosses her arms over her chest and taps her foot on the ground. "That's not an answer."

It shouldn't matter. I've governed demons, brokered empires. I've stared the worst of humanity in the eye and never blinked.

But her standing there, tapping her foot, makes me want to tell her everything my heart desires and more. It also makes me love her more.

"We're soulmarked. That is fate. But it begins the path—it does not finish it. The next step is the infernal claim." I decide to just get that part over with.

She looks at me with the most adorable scrunched face. She's confused. I may need to explain this very slowly. Break it down for her.

"It is what mortals would call...consummation," I say.

Her face is flushing all over again. "You mean—"

"Yes," I answer to save her from finishing that sentence.

"What about marriage?" She asks. "Do demons even get married?"

"The claim, or consummation is first, then the Infernal Union," I explain. "The union is our version of a wedding."

"Another wedding," she groans.

"One of your choice. You get to do the planning this time," I chuckle.

She swallows. "If we do nothing?"

I meet her eyes. "We remain as we are. Soulmarked. Undone. There is no punishment. Only longing."

"So... in Hell," she murmurs, "you seal your bond by... by laying together."

"Yes."

"Before marriage."

"Marriage is a mortal construct," I say. "A contract made in front of witnesses. Often broken. Often meaningless."

Her expression falters. But she doesn't look away. I'll give her that. Defiant and strong. She wants a wedding though.

"The Claim is for us. The Union is before the Infernal Council. It is made in truth. In blood. In will. It is not 'before' anything. It is the beginning."

I let the words settle between us. She doesn't speak, but her pulse has quickened. I can feel it.

"Let's do it," she says.

I choke on air and begin to cough. I'm sure that she doesn't understand what she's saying. "What do you mean?"

"The Claim," she clarifies, lifting her chin. "I want it. I want…"

She exhales. Her eyes flicker—hope, fear, defiance—all crashing around the calm she's trying to portray.

She shakes her head, like even *she* can't believe what she's admitting.

"I want to be chosen. Wanted. Not traded or married off like a tool. I want to belong somewhere—*to someone*—and know it wasn't stolen or arranged. I want love."

She doesn't want to be claimed alone. She wants more. To be seen, heard, and respected. Not just bought.

"And I think…" she pauses. "I think I could love you. Eventually. And I think you'd know what to do with it if I did."

Something in my chest pulls taut—painful, sharp, *honest*.

I rise slowly, letting the silence stretch. "You would not be chosen like an offering," I tell her. "You would be claimed like a miracle."

Her breath stutters.

I reach for her—not rushing. Not demanding. Just offering.

"Say the word," I whisper. "And the world will feel it."

"I want it. I want you," she says.

The words hit like a spark down my spine. I stay still for a breath. Just one. Watching her. Letting the moment wrap around us like a thread pulled tight.

I rise from the couch, every inch of me focused on her. Her eyes follow the movement like she can feel what's coming.

I cross the space between us, stopping just close enough to let the heat pass between our bodies without touching. One hand slips into her hair, curling around the nape of her neck. I tilt her face up.

"Liora," I murmur. "This is your choice. Your word holds the gate."

She doesn't hesitate. "I'm saying yes."

That's all I need. I kiss her deeply. I want to memorize the shape of her breath against mine. She responds with a softness that turns to hunger fast—her fingers bunching in my shirt, dragging me closer like she wants all of me now.

I scoop her into my arms. She lets out a startled gasp, but her legs curl instinctively around me, her breath warm against my throat.

I carry her through the estate's long hall—dim light flickering over stone, everything silent but her heartbeat and mine.

When we reach the master bedroom, I don't fumble. I don't rush. I set her down gently on the edge of the bed.

But I don't step back. My hands stay on her hips. My mouth hovers near hers.

Her breath hitches and I feel her tremble between us.

She lifts her eyes to mine, uncertain, but not afraid.

"This will be my first time," she says, barely above a whisper.

I incline my head. "I know."

I'm curious to see what she says. I want to know everything about her. What's going through her head.

She swallows, fingers curling lightly into the fabric at my chest. "Does that... trouble you?"

"Not in the least," I murmur, brushing a knuckle along the curve of her cheek. "It honors me."

I kiss her gently—once at the corner of her mouth, then again along her jaw, just beneath her ear. Her breath catches, her lashes lowering like a curtain.

"You're not just offering your body," I say, my voice low, "but your trust. That is no small thing."

"I only wish to feel certain. To feel... right."

"You will." My thumb lingers at the edge of her lips. "This night will be what you wish it to be—nothing more, nothing less."

She lets out a breath that trembles with something between relief and anticipation.

"You are very sure of yourself," she says, half-smiling.

"Not of myself," I reply, "but of *you*."

I kiss her again, more deeply, letting her feel my restraint—how much I hold back for her sake.

Her hands come to rest against my chest. Hesitant at first. Then braver.

"What if I do something... wrong?"

"There is no wrong," I say softly. "There is only what you desire, and what you do not."

She laughs, the sound light and a little breathless. Keeping my eyes on hers, I take her hands in mine, guiding them to the fastenings of my coat.

She hesitates. Her eyes are wide and vulnerable. "Are you certain?"

I bring my forehead to hers, the warmth of her skin grounding me.

"I have waited lifetimes for what you offer freely. " My voice drops. "You are a gift."

I stand her up from the bed. The firelight traces her skin as I peel the coat I gave her from her shoulders. She lets it fall without a word—but the moment she's in nothing but her shift, her arms cross over her chest.

"Don't look at me like that," she murmurs.

"Like what?" I ask, stepping close.

Her brows pull together. "Like I'm... more."

I reach out, gently easing her arms away.

"You are."

She doesn't look away, but I see the war behind her eyes—wanting to be seen, and fearing what it means.

I press a kiss to her forehead. Next, her cheek. Then her collarbone. Each one slower than the last.

"Let me worship you," I whisper. "Or I'll kneel until you ask me to."

That makes her breath hitch. Her hands uncurl.

I guide her gently to the bed once again. Lay her back. Unlace her stays with the patience of a man who knows he's not just undoing a garment—he's undoing every thread of fear stitched into her.

When I bare her to the firelight, she flinches again. My hands find hers. And when she lets me kiss her again, she doesn't hold back.

I lower myself over her, kissing her breast softly, then with purpose—tongue flicking over the peak, drawing a gasp from her throat. Her back arches, uncertain and instinctive, but god, she *responds*.

My hand trails down her belly, between her thighs. She's already slick—already trembling. I tease her, just once, my thumb brushing over the bundle of nerves hidden there, and she jerks like I've set her alight.

"Evander—"

"I've got you," I whisper, pressing a kiss to her hip. "Let go for me."

I slide one finger into her, slow and deep, curling slightly until her breath stutters. She tightens around me, wet and wanting, and her hand flies to my wrist like she doesn't know whether to pull me away or press me closer.

Her head tips back as I move inside her, patient and steady, coaxing her higher. Her thighs shake. Her lips part. She moans—quietly, like she's not used to making noise.

"You don't have to hold anything back." My voice is rough now, frayed at the edges. "Let me hear you."

And god, she does. She falls apart around my fingers, hips rising, breath ragged, a choked cry leaving her lips as her release takes her under.

I don't give her time to drift. I move over her, catch her mouth in mine, and kiss her hard.

"Bone of my bone," I murmur against her lips, "breath of my breath."

She trembles—eyes locked on mine, lips parted.

"Invite me, then," she whispers, "rapture then alone must reign... and scenes confess how dear the conquest was to gain."

"Alexander Pope," I say, voice hushed.

She nods, just once. "It felt right."

"It is." I press my forehead to hers. "It's perfect."

I line myself up, and when I push into her, I do it slowly.

She's impossibly tight and her breath hitches, a soft sound that breaks around the edges. Her hands clutch the sheets, eyes squeezed shut. She's trying to be brave.

I still, only halfway inside of her. "Liora. Open your eyes, Dove."

She opens her eyes and looks at me. They're wet, but not angry.

"I'm alright," she whispers. "I just didn't know it would feel like that."

I lower myself to kiss her brow, my hand smoothing over her cheek. "I can stop."

She shakes her head. "I want to continue."

I shift and move, only stopping only when I'm fully inside her.

She trembles.

"You feel—" she can't even say it.

"So do you," I growl, resting my forehead against hers.

I wait. And when she nods, just once, I begin to move.

Slow strokes. Deep, grinding rhythm. My hand tangled in her hair, her legs wrapped around me.

She meets me with every thrust, soft moans spilling into my neck, her nails raking my back.

I don't hold back. Not now.

I worship her with my mouth, my hands, my body.

And when she clenches around me, another climax stealing her breath, I follow with a groan, hips pressing deep as I spill inside her.

The Claim ignites. My mark flares gold, bright enough to alight the space between us. When hers responds, it's just as beautiful.

The room thrums with power, the air shimmering as magic seals between us—body and soul.

She's panting beneath me, dazed and flushed, her skin glowing faintly in the firelight.

We stay in bed—wrapped in fur and each other, limbs tangled. She rests her cheek on my chest, fingers idly tracing the mark between my ribs. It's golden now. But it hums when she touches it.

She hums, a soft, content sound. "I can't feel where I end and you begin."

"That's the point, dove."

Her laugh is sleepy and satisfied. She shifts, stretches like a cat beneath the furs, and ends up straddling my waist, hair a wild halo.

"You didn't say I'd be this sore," she mutters, mock accusatory.

I rest my hands lightly on her hips. "Should I apologize?"

She leans down, bracing herself against my chest, her lips brushing my ear. "Not unless you plan on doing it again."

There's a challenge in her eyes now. One I'm more than willing to lose to.

She rolls her hips once and a low groan catches in the back of my throat.

"Liora," I rasp.

"Lie back," she says.

I listen to her. She takes her time this round—her rhythm, her pace, her power.

When I'm finally undone beneath her, she kisses me like I'm hers. Because I am.

We spend the next week or so in bed more often than not.Getting to know each other, body and soul. But now it's time to go to Hell. I want to show her my home. My world. Meet my brother and sister-in-law.

"Dove..." I rub her back as I try to wake her. "I want to take you somewhere."

She's up immediately, her eyes brightening and shoulders pulled back. "I'm ready."

I laugh softly, pressing a kiss to her shoulder as I help her with her stays, lacing them with less haste than the first time.

She tightens her gloves with a snap. "What's your brother like?"

"Difficult. Brilliant. Viciously loyal." I grin. "You'll like each other too much."

We're gone in minutes—through a portal threaded with infernal sigils—and the moment we step through, the world changes.

Obsidian streets under twilight skies, carved towers that shimmer like polished bone, and a thrum beneath it all—like power waiting to be named.

This is Hell.

My everything. Until now.

Theron's home is carved into black cliffs, half-suspended above a river of lightless water. Massive iron gates part as we step through, the runes on them glowing faintly at our presence. Inside, it's all black stone lit by ever-burning sconces of cold flame.

Liora takes it in with wide eyes. She doesn't look scared or nervous for that matter. That takes me by surprise. I would have thought she would be intimidated, but here she is...enjoying every moment.

We reach the front entrance. Before I can turn the handle, the doors swing open.

Theron stands in the threshold, arms crossed, amber eyes cool and calculating.

He takes one look at Liora and smirks. "So you're the girl who's been haunting my brother?"

Liora doesn't miss a beat. "I am. Although, that's an odd way to introduce yourself to someone who loves your brother."

His smirk twitches into something faintly amused. His eyes twinkle and he gives me a look of approval.

Selene steps beside him—barefoot in layered black silk, auburn curls loose around her shoulders, silver eyes sharp and impossible to read.

She studies Liora with the kind of stillness that makes demons confess.

"He's bad at hellos," she says. "I'm Selene. That's Theron. You must be Liora."

I've told them about her, through the bond we share as brothers. I haven't been able to stop myself from going on and on about her endlessly. I know Selene feels like they're already great friends.

Liora nods, steady as ever. "I am."

Selene's lips quirk. "You're exactly how I pictured you."

Liora arches a brow, then looks to me. "Is that good or bad?"

"Both," Selene answers, without missing a beat. "It means Evander here has told Theron almost everything already."

Theron steps aside, giving us just enough room to pass.

Selene looks her over and smiles like she's already guessed the ending of a story no one else has read. "You carry yourself like you know exactly who you are."

Liora meets her gaze. "I always have, my parents allowed me that freedom"

That makes Selene's smile widen, just slightly.

"You've got a backbone," Theron mutters. "Let's hope it holds."

"Yours seems intact," Liora replies. "So I'm not worried."

He huffs a soft laugh and finally steps aside, giving us room to pass.

"She's mouthy," he says.

"She's observant," Selene corrects.

We step into the sitting room—cool stone, velvet-backed chairs, and a silver flame flickering low in the hearth gives me a sense of comfort. Selene sinks gracefully into a chaise, one leg tucked beneath her.

Liora stays standing.

"So…" she begins, glancing between them. "How did you two meet?"

Theron lifts a brow. "Nosy."

"Curious," Liora corrects. "There's a difference."

Selene exhales through a smile. "Salem."

Liora straightens a little. "As in… the town that held the witch trials in the United States?"

"The very one," Selene says, reaching for a glass of dark wine. "I was human then. The town thought I was dangerous."

"Were you?"

Selene tips her head, a smirk growing on her face. "Not yet."

Theron watches her the way a man does when he still hasn't gotten over how she looked that first night. "Our father made a deal with her. Thought she was just another clever mortal with a mouth too sharp for her own good."

Selene cuts him a glance. "He was right."

Liora blinks. "So your father took her soul?" I'm glad I'd filled her in on the broader details of what my family does. If not, she'd be lost and probably horrified at this conversation.

"Tried to," Theron says. "Didn't realize she'd already bargained it away herself."

Selene shrugs, unapologetic. "I had reasons. None of them noble. But I never asked for salvation. I asked for sovereignty."

Her gaze shifts back to Liora, steady and unapologetic. "When they came for me with ropes and prayers, Theron was the only one who didn't flinch."

"I killed eight Puritans that night," Theron says, deadpan.

"He made it look like an accident." Selene smiles at her mate.

"They fell on pitchforks." He shrugged, a satisfied look on his face.

Selene's lips curl. "After that, I followed him into Hell."

Liora is quiet for a moment. Just watching them. "That's... romantic."

"It's a little screwed up," Selene replies. "But so are we."

Liora's voice is soft when she speaks. "Do you ever miss the world above?"

Selene leans her head against the back of her chair, gaze on the flickering silver flames. "Sometimes. But I don't miss who I was in it."

Theron doesn't answer. He never does when the past gets brought up. But his silence says enough.

Selene rises from her seat and drifts toward the door. "I like her," she says, not looking back. "Don't ruin it."

"He won't," Liora says, before I can speak.

Theron trails after his mate, muttering, "We'll see."

It's finally just the two of us again. Liora leans into me, her head on my shoulder.

"I'm still learning," she murmurs. "But I think I could love this place. As long as you're in it."

I kiss her temple, slow and certain. "You'll love it completely because I'm never leaving you."

This isn't just the beginning of her descent.

It's the beginning of her belonging.

Chapter Eight
Liora

The moment the portal disappears around us, I realize I have been holding my breath the whole time.

I am not good at meeting new people...clearly. But there's just something about being seen. Not as a duchess or a pawn in someone else's bigger game. Not a virgin bride. Just me.

There was no ulterior motive or pretend friendliness. They didn't make excuses to hear more about my family's connection to the king or status. Nothing boring or unnatural.

We were taught to fear demons. That going to Hell is a horrific end if you don't act or behave a certain way. Priests preach torture and pain.

"What's going through that active mind of yours?" Evander asks. I shake my head and turn to him. I didn't even notice we were on a bustling road until now.

"I guess I got trapped in my own head," I say, sighing as I lean in his embrace.

"We can go back to my house if you'd like," he says. "Hell will still be here later, we have all the time in the world to explore."

I instantly perk up. I want to know more about my new home. This place. I'm not scared. I look at all the faces around me and realize that I don't stand out, at least not in the way I'm used to.

The only reason I do is because I'm just in Evander's coat and my stays. No one seems to notice though. I look down. *I can't wait to get out of these clothes.*

"I thought we could come to the market place first," Evander says. "Maybe you can find something you'd like to wear. Eventually, I'll teach you how to make your own clothes."

I look at him questioningly. I have never been good at sewing. I tried. I'm awful. My tutor used to laugh and tell me that I was lucky to be born in the position that I was, that I'd never make it in the 'real' world as she called it.

Yvette tried to teach me once—said every lady should know how to mend a tear or stitch a hem. The dress I tried to alter came out more mangled than anything resembling clothing.

Yvette laughed until she cried. I haven't touched a needle since.

My displeasure must be all over my face because he starts to laugh.

"No, Dove," he says, still chuckling. "Just think about what you want to wear and it'll appear."

I think about it. I don't want to embarrass him so I turn to look at what the women are wearing around me. Really look and really watch.

I feel Evander wrap his arms around my waist and put his lips to the shell of my ear. "Don't worry about what others have on. What do you want?"

What do *I* want to wear? Not what my mother would have chosen or Yvette. Not any stylist. Not what Paris expects. I don't have to walk around and see some noblewoman on her third husband nod at me in approval.

I close my eyes and wrack my brain. I want something that moves. Nothing stiff. I like being able to breathe...and eat. I want dark colors that shimmer in the firelight.

As soon as I picture it, I will it to be.

It's a dress. But not just any dress. A black one layered in this soft, light fabric. It has no name. Probably because it doesn't exist. Not really anyway.

The bodice fits like a second skin, embroidered with constellations in thread that shifts from silver to shadow with every step. There are no stays. No hooks. No one had to lace me into it.

My hair lifts with the magic, moving like it knows exactly where it needs to go. Dark, loose waves fall on my shoulders with half of it twisting up. There is no powder or pins. No forcing it into a certain shape. No wigs. All natural and all me.

I think about my face and what I want my cosmetics to be. Not painted or smeared. Darkened lips like ripe berries. Some kohl on my eyes makes them appear longer and wider. I keep my natural flush, not putting powder all over.

Evander's breath catches behind me. "There you are."

"What do you mean?"

He steps closer. "This isn't a disguise. It isn't a performance. This... is you. The version you were never allowed to become."

His gaze drags over me. He looks at me like I am desirable and he could just slip my clothes off right here, right now. "The you that was always meant to be."

He grabs my hand and we begin to walk. When we step through the wrought-iron archway, my breath hitches in my throat. It's beautiful.

"Come," he says. "It's time you saw the world you've entered."

We step into what I can assume is the city proper. I look at the sky. It's not dark. Almost like twilight never goes away. The obsidian streets gleam under the stars, somehow bright despite the faint glow of a sunset. The buildings are twisted and rhythmic. The outside as glowing letters...or words that I can't read. They're twisting around the outside like poetry.

"This is the Obsidian Wards," he says. "Kind of like the heart of Hell. Those glowing things are runes."

I try to study everything, but there was a sudden movement. The places around us start to move.

"Are we going through another portal?" I ask.

"No," Evander says as we keep walking. "The city can feel you and only those with intention can walk without getting lost. Hell is a never ending universe. Its vastness is how people get lost."

We pass markets that I can't fully see, they're in my peripheral vision, but when I try to focus on them, they're gone. I know they're there, though. The scent of something that doesn't seem normal, the sound of hawkers selling their wares, it gives the sensation that anything can be sold. A stall draped in velvet is selling dragon's saliva.

I pull on Evander's hand and lift a brow at him. I tilt my head at the stall. "Dragons?"

Evander glances at the stall, then back at me with a crooked smile.

"Not dragons. Just overcompensation in a bottle." He tugs me a little closer. "Some idiot once dreamed them into existence here—now we've got peddlers selling the memory of having wings and breathing fire."

Good to know that even demons can be a strange bunch.

"What is this place?"

"Veil Market," Evander replies. "Neutral ground. No contracts and no battles."

A demon woman brushes past me, her eyes silver. "Excuse me."

They have better manners than most aristocrats.

We reach a courtyard. It is wreathed in pale flame. Stone statues of what looks like demons line the path. They are fear inducing—some weeping, some laughing, all too lifelike.

"This is the Bone Garden," he murmurs. "Where demons come to mourn what they lost."

"Lost? Like a cemetary?" I am surprised. I shouldn't be. Of course they have one. But I thought they were immortal.

"Specifically from the rebellion."

"That means—that your parents are here," I say.

"They are," he affirms.

"I'm sorry," I say.

He doesn't say anything. We move on from the Bone Garden.

"The Court of the Unseen," he says. "Where deals are judged, sealed... or broken."

He doesn't linger. Instead, we move toward a path lit by floating lanterns, their light soft and golden, as if powered by hope instead of heat.

"The Ember Paths," he says. "They lead to the outer realms. And beyond that..."

I look up at him. "What?"

"My home," he says, smirking.

The path curves into the cliffside, carved smooth by time and magic. The rock isn't jagged but veined—threads of silver and violet pulsing beneath the surface like they're under skin. It's alive, in the way everything in Hell seems to be.

Below, the chasm stretches wide and endless, filled not with fire but mist—soft and thick, like spilled silk. Occasionally, shapes move through it. As if the cliff is reading bedtime stories to children.

Far in the distance, spires rise like teeth from the stone. Glowing windows, hanging bridges, the hum of ancient languages.

Evander's home is built into that curve. As if it belongs there. As if *he* belongs there.

We pass through a low arch and move towards a dim hallway.

The walls are smooth—almost black—but not glossy. The floor is polished but unadorned, and I notice there are no rugs. Shelves line one side of the room, carved directly into the wall, holding books in languages I don't know, and a few items that don't look like they're meant to be touched.

I walk slowly, fingertips brushing the spine of a book I can't read. There's no dust. No clutter. No place for either.

There's a table in the center of the room—long and pale, not white exactly, but something close. Maybe bone. Maybe glass. It gleams faintly, but not in a decorative way. It's the only thing here that doesn't look like it belongs.

"This belonged to my father," he says. "He made it for my mother as an infernal union present."

My chest aches at the words, although I know it will happen one day, I can't imagine losing my parents. My dad had always let me be who I was, so did my mom. They faltered with that marriage contract, but up until then, they let me be...me. I trace the edge of the table again—something softer than bone, cooler than glass, shaped by a love that wanted to hold forever.

"Theron and I—" he pauses. "We used to sit around this table at night. Listen to mother tell stories. She'd sit right there—" he nods to the high-backed chair at the head, "and call it her throne."

"What kind of stories?" I ask softly.

He smiles, but it's faint.

"She used to tell us about her infernal union. About how my father carved this table with his own hands. How he didn't offer her flowers or jewels, but this—a place for their future. A place that would outlast them both."

A breath catches in my throat.

"She told it like it was a fairytale," he murmurs. "There is so much beauty in Hell that we haven't discovered yet.. That we need to be thankful to be surrounded by something so sacred."

I don't speak. I can't.

He lowers himself into one of the chairs, his eyes tracing the table-top like it might still hold her reflection.

"But she didn't believe in happy endings. Not really." He pauses. "Because love like theirs doesn't survive revolutions."

I draw in a shaky breath.

"I wasn't there," he says, and every damned edge of his holds something I can't unsee. "Theron was. He watched them fall. Together. Holding hands."

I press my free hand to my throat, unable to stop the tears that slip down like quiet absolution.

They had built peace. And Hell burned it down.

He exhales, ragged. "For a long time, I believed love was a story we inherited, not one we got to live. That it always ended in fire. That choosing someone meant losing them."

His eyes stay fixed on the table. Like if he looks at me, the dam will break.

"I watched Theron shut himself off. Closed and cruel. And then... Selene."

There's something like awe in his voice. "She scared him. He loved that. She didn't flinch. She *chose* him with her own free will. I saw the way he softened when he thought no one was looking."

He finally looks at me.

"I started to wonder... if love could survive anything. Not just Hell. The darkness. The damage."

His voice falters.

"I'm not afraid of you, Liora," he says, barely more than a whisper. "I'm afraid of what I'd become without you. That I'd survive centuries again and never feel like this. Not once."

My throat tightens. I swallow it down.

"I'm not leaving," I say.

He studies me for a long beat. "Don't make promises you can't—"

"I'm not," I interrupt firmly. "You didn't ask me to follow. I chose to. And I don't choose lightly."

His breath hitches, just once. He doesn't speak. But his grip tightens like he's afraid the moment might slip through.

I won't let it.

So I rise onto my toes and kiss him. His lips part in surprise, just enough for me to catch his bottom lip between mine.

That's all it takes.

His control snaps like a thread pulled too tight. His hands fly to my waist, dragging me closer until there's not a breath between us. He kisses me back like he's been starved for centuries and I'm the only thing that's ever tasted like hope.

It's messy. Desperate. His mouth slants over mine again and again, until I'm gasping against him, clutching his shoulders like I might fall.

He groans low in his throat, then lifts me, pushing me until my back meets the nearest wall. Its cold stone at my spine makes me shiver, while my lips are on fire.

I laugh, breathless. He swallows the sound with another kiss.

"You're dangerous like this," he murmurs.

"Good," I manage, tugging his hair to pull him back down. "Then maybe we're even."

His eyes flash with something fierce. He kisses me again, not slowing down. I can feel how much he wants me and I want him all of the same.

Once we pull apart, he puts me on the ground, our eyes connected and we stay in each other's arms for a while—two souls who were never promised peace, but are daring to believe they deserve it anyway.

Chapter Nine
Evander

My Infernal Union. Theron is standing with me as I finish getting ready. Liora has planned this event down to the most miniscule of details.

"Are you ready?" Theron brushes some imaginary lint off of my shoulders.

"Of course," I say, turning to look at him, raising a brow.

He tilts his head, studying me like he's looking inside me. Maybe trying to figure out if I'm lying.

"I felt the same way you do now," he says.

I look back to the mirror, straightening my tie for the tenth time. "What way is that?"

"That you wish they were here to witness this," he says.

The words hit harder than I expect. I feel that familiar ache grow and harden in my chest. That gaping hole that never seems to dissipate when I think about them.

Theron's eyes shift to the wall behind me. A glazed look in his eyes. He's thinking about them too.

"I used to picture her," he says. "Our mother. Sitting in the front row. Wearing that deep violet she said brought out her eyes. Tears of joy streaming down her face. She never wept loudly—just let them gracefully fall as she smiled through them."

I turn away from him to cover the tears silently falling. I try to wipe them away, but can't catch them quick enough. We never discussed their death. They missed his union too. I try to blink away the moisture as best I can.

"Father," he continues. A breath of laughter almost escapes his lips. I look back at him. "He'd have stood too close, ruined the formality with some badly timed line about how fate had mercy on us with our mate's infernal beauty."

I don't know whether to laugh or sob. The sound that comes out of my throat sounds a bit like both.

"They would have loved her," he says, looking into my eyes. "Liora. From the moment she opened her mouth."

I nod, but it's a struggle.

"They should be here."

Theron turns, running his hand through his hair. He starts to pace back and forth.

"I think about it more than I care to admit," he says. "The rebellion. The pit. Them pushed into it."

He sighs and stops pacing all at once.

"If fate hadn't intervened, they would still be here," he says, his voice cracking slightly. "It should've been me. Not them."

"No," I say firmly. "They were murdered because the realm feared change. Because the cowards couldn't fathom love as power. Not because of you. And not because of Selene."

I've carried it so long," he whispers. "The shame."

He exhales, unsteady. A single tear slips down his cheek. He lets it.

"I miss them," I say, voice rough. "Every day. But I see them in us. In the way we keep fighting. In the way we love."

Theron swipes his hand over his face, then straightens.

"They'd be proud," he says. "Of you."

I nod, swallowing hard. "Thank you."

"No," he says. "Thank you for not letting the past define you. For choosing to hope anyway."

We stand there, two sons in mourning, on the edge of something new.

There is a knock at the door. "Enter."

Henri and Marguerite step into the room, dressed in what Liora designed. Marguerite's gown is dark silver laced with midnight blue. Henry's coat is deep forest green, trimmed in subtle gold. They look regal, but not like mortal royalty.

Henri is the first to speak.

"You're not our blood," he says. "But today, if you'll have us, we'd be honored to stand with you as if you were."

I blink. My throat tightens instantly.

Marguerite smiles, stepping closer. "Liora told us what she could... about the war. About your parents."

She doesn't ask for more. Doesn't prod at the wounds that never closed.

"But whatever you lost," she says softly, "you don't have to go through today alone."

I glance at Theron. He's staring straight ahead, jaw clenched.

Marguerite's gaze softens even more. "We've loved Liora since the moment she came into this world. And now she's chosen you. That's enough for us."

Henri steps beside her, his hand warm on my shoulder. "Let us be proud of you today. Let us stand in that space."

For a moment, all I can do is nod. My voice wouldn't work even if I tried.

Theron finally murmurs, "They would've liked you."

Henry lets out a quiet breath. "Then we'll try to be worthy of the memory."

The four of us leave the room we are in to walk to the large church. Only Liora would be able to find a sacred pavillion this beautiful in the middle of Hell.

She has made so many friends here that there are no demons on earth. Or in any other areas of Hell. Everyone wanted to come.

The obsidian doors groan open, and I step into the main chamber. Row after row of demons and their mates fill every available corner.

As I reach the front, the seven figures of the Infernal Council tower beneath the stained glass. Their cloaks ripple around them in unison.

They have no eye—or faces for that matter. Their hoods are up and the darkness that surrounds where their face should be is a black hole.

They speak—not one by one, but together. A single voice from seven mouths. Ageless. Resonant.

"Evander Duvain. Do you come of your own will, with your soul unclouded and purpose true?"

"I do."

"Do you accept what is asked—that once given, love cannot be undone, nor soul unbound?"

"I do."

Their hoods incline slightly, a gesture more ancient than nodding.

One of the cloaked figures tilts its head—subtly, but toward me. A voice rises again, but this time it isn't spoken aloud. It threads directly into my mind.

"Cassian and Serenya left behind more than blood, Evander Duvain. They left belief."

The others remain still, unmoving.

"Your mother's final words were of you. My boys will love well, and truly. And that will be their legacy."

My throat tightens. I can't move. Can't breathe.

"Your father said nothing—but he held her hand." A pause. Gentle. Grieving. "They died together. For peace. For you."

The great doors at the end of the hall groan open once again. I stop breathing completely when I see Liora standing at the end of what now seems like an impossibly long aisle. I've never seen anything like it, and I'm sure I never will again.

She's bathed in twilight and shadows, framed by the black marble arch, with her arm looped through her father's.

Her gown isn't white. It's deeper than pearl, shimmering with faint undertones of starlight and smoke. Layers of silk and moonlit gauze trail behind her. The train moves like it's alive, beating with her heartbeat.

A crown—not of gold, but of woven infernal glass—rests lightly atop her head. Her hair is swept back in soft waves, pinned with silver threads that catch the light like fireflies.

Her eyes find mine.

This is not the girl I found behind Parisian walls. This is a queen. A force.

My mate.

We stand before the Council.

One raises a skeletal hand. "Speak your truth. Bind your fates."

I take her hands in mine.

"Liora," I say, voice wavering slightly around the edges, "I have walked through fire and ruin. I have faced centuries of pain. But none of it taught me how to live—not until you. I vow to stand beside you. To listen. To follow, where you lead. To be yours—not in domination, but in devotion. I am not your captor. I am your chosen."

She blinks fast. Her fingers tighten in mine.

She lifts her chin, voice strong. "Evander. I was born into duty. Raised for a crown I never chose. But you—you offered me choice. You asked for nothing but my yes. So I give it freely. I give it fiercely. I vow to love you not with obedience, but with passion. With truth. With the strength you saw in me before I saw it myself. You are not my fate. You are my freedom."

She pauses, but I know she has more to say. She's going through every poem or story she has ever read for the perfect one for this moment.

"I loved you first: but afterwards your love, outsoaring mine, sang such a loftier song. As drowned the friendly cooings of my dove. Christina Rossetti," she murmurs.

"The perfect poem for the perfect moment, Dove," I say, chuckling.

The Council speaks as one. "Then so it is written. So it shall burn."

Magic surges between us—body, soul, eternity.

I pull her into my arms. Our mouths meet. We are no longer two.

We are bound.

Infernal. Eternal.

One.

After the ceremony, everyone went to our house for a party. I thought maybe only a few would be there, but it turns out everyone wanted to join.

Every inch of the house is full to the brim.

Liora is walking around and chatting with people. She's glowing, her smile lighting up every face, every dark corner around her.

"I need to talk to you," Henri says, coming up behind me.

I turn, unable to wipe the smile off of my own face. His expression is the complete opposite of his daughters. Where hers is pure joy, his is serious, stonelike. He waits until we're a few steps away from the others before speaking.

"The De Launays have been exiled from court," Henri says, his voice low but firm. "They didn't just lose favor—they were cast out. Titles stripped. Holdings seized. Their name removed from every ledger and court document as though it never carried weight at all."

He pauses, looking around to see if his wife or Liora are listening. "Philippe tried to argue, of course. Claimed breach of promise. But the court wouldn't hear it. When I made it clear the crown would never align with men who enjoy those who sell their daughters like livestock for their own gain. Apparently we were not the first family that the de Launays tried this with. We weren't even the third. But we were the first fools. Not anymore. I made sure the rest of nobility followed suit.They're pariahs now. The scandal alone has scorched their legacy. No invitations. No allies. Their downfall was swift and absolute."

"They got what they deserved in a mortal sense, but they are not absolved completely," I say. "Hell has a way of taking what's owed. More will happen soon enough."

Henry smiles into his glass. I can tell that he likes that idea. For everything that family did to his daughter. They deserve to sit on the edge of their seats until they experience what true peril feels like.

Liora comes to me and wraps her arms around my waist. She smiles at me like I'm her beginning and end. Her everything.

She melts into me the moment our lips meet. The cheers around us blur into a distant hum. My hand cradles the back of her neck, her fingers clutch my shirt, and for a breathless instant, it's just the two of us.

It may have started with elevating a place in court. Duty. What others desired.

But it ends with peace. With Belonging. With a love fierce enough to shake the stars—and eternal enough to outlast them.

Epilogue
Liora

I t's been nearly two months since the Infernal Union. My parents arrived yesterday for a visit—just a few days, they said. We've kept the guest room ready, though I think they just wanted a little more time with us.

I couldn't be happier.

Evander got called away to make a deal. Selene told me that happens often, but they're never gone for long. Not when they have their mates waiting for them at home.

When he gets back, he's going to take my parents home and he'll teach me how to use that portal thing to see them whenever I want.

My mom is in the kitchen drinking some tea with my father when I walk in.

"Good morning, darling," she says.

Selene is cooking something. Whatever it is that smells divine.

"What is that?"

"Rabbit braised in cream and mustard. Your mother said it's your favorite," Selene says.

I get closer to take a sniff. And instantly freeze. My face goes pale. Everything in me is telling me I'm about to be ill.

"Oh—no. No, no, no." I turn gagging. "It smells like boiled feet! What did you do to it?"

"Nothing! I followed the recipe exactly," Selene says, looking at the recipe card confused.

I stumble back and cover my mouth. "Why does it smell sour?"

My father is laughing at this point. "Your mother couldn't stand rabbit either. Or cream. Or mustard."

I stare at him. *What does he mean? What could she not stand?*

"When she was with child," he finishes.

With child? That's impossible. Well maybe not fully impossible, but it can't be! I stare at my father like he just sprouted horns.

"Congratulations! Try not to vomit on the carpet," Selene says, grinning.

"Why would Liora vomit at all?" Evander asks from behind me.

I can't even process answering. I don't even know what he said. Or what to say to him.

"Seems like our Liora here is with child," Selene says.

I barely flinch. I think it's starting to sink in. The nausea has passed. But hearing it out loud makes it that much more real.

"We're going to have a child," he whispers. It sounds like his dream is coming true. We never even discussed it.

"We must have a party," my mother says. Her voice is high and sweet, filled with so much uncontained joy. "To celebrate this beautiful event."

My father chuckles, brushing a hand against hers.

"We just had a party, my dear," my father says, smiling at my mother.

I sit back, letting their voices rise around me—celebration blooming like jasmine in summer heat.

I press my palm over my stomach again.

Not entirely mine anymore. There is something more there. A child that I am growing.

I didn't plan for this. But not everything precious is planned. Some things are given. This one...this one I will keep.

The worst pain I've ever felt rips right through my body.

It's nothing like I've felt the last couple of days. Not a fluttering or tightness. Pressure blooms low and wide. All through my pelvis all the way up my spine.

A loud groan rips through me as I grab my stomach.

"Dove—" Evander starts.

"Get Thalia," I tell him.

Within seconds, Thalia, Hell's midwife extraordinaire comes in.

Thalia Endora. Born on Delos, in 431 BCE. Raised in a temple to Artemis and Apollo, trained to bring life into the world with ritual, with herbcraft, with songs older than language.

Her mate, Kael, works deep in the lower wards, binding soul-ribbons, preserving memory like it's sacred. She speaks of him often. I saw the way her hand brushed the ribbon on her wrist when she talked about him. That said enough.

She looks like she stepped out of marble and memory—barefoot, robed in indigo draped silk, silver thread gleaming in soft curves across her shoulders. Her dark curls are coiled and pinned with carved bone, and her bronze gold eyes cut straight through panic.

Evander stands frozen near the door, jaw locked, red eyes wide—not with fear, exactly, but with a kind of helpless fury.

Thalia doesn't even look at me first. She walks straight up to him.

"You may be the greatest dealmaker alive, but I was delivering heirs when Sparta still stood. When the first king of Athens was born screaming in a storm—I caught him myself."

Evander opens his mouth. She lifts a single finger.

"Go to her. Or leave. You will not pace. You will not command."

He moves straight to me, grabbing my hand.

"Come, Liora. Bed, now. Let me work," Thalia says.

Evander lifts me and takes me to the bedroom, laying me down.

She pulls back the sheets with one hand and places the other on my abdomen. Her fingers are warm as she pats my shoulder.

"You're further along than I expected," she says calmly. "But not too far. We'll do this here. Now."

Another contraction hits. This one takes me by the spine and *shoves*.

I bite back a scream and turn into Evander's chest instead. He's kneeling beside the bed now, both hands in mine, eyes burning like coals trying not to flare.

"You're strong, Dove," he whispers. "You're everything."

"Liora. Focus on your breathing. You don't have to fight this," Thalia interjects.

The pain isn't linear—it spirals. Presses. I feel like I'm being torn open and remade at the same time.

The world begins to shift. Then, in the blink of an eye, something shifts. Sharp and sudden. The pressure builds until I can't feel anything but white hot pain.

"It's time," Thalia says. "You're ready."

Evander stays at my side.

His hand is wrapped in mine—tight enough that I know I'm hurting him, but he doesn't flinch. He just keeps whispering. Little things. My name. Promises. That I'm doing well. That he's here.

Thalia kneels between my legs, sleeves rolled, face steady. The runes on her arms shimmer faintly now, activated by sweat and blood and breath. She's not panicking. Not even close.

"Breathe when I say. Push when I say. That's all you need to do." She's done this before. Too many times to count.

Another contraction builds—harder this time. My entire body locks. I'm not ready. It doesn't matter.

"Now," Thalia says.

I scream this time.

Not because I want to—but because the air needs somewhere to go. Because the pressure is unbearable. Because power is leaving me in a way that has nothing to do with magic and everything to do with becoming a mother to my child.

Evander brushes sweat from my temple. His hand shakes.

"You're almost there," he says, voice hoarse.

I believe him. But I don't have time to respond. Another contraction—this one knocks the breath from my lungs.

The threads above me flare, burning gold and silver and red. They twist and knot in midair, as if the future itself is bracing.

"One more, Liora," Thalia says, voice low and sure. "Push."

I push one more time, face turning red and body tightening. I clench every muscle that I have and feel the fire burning within me.

I hear a cry. It's not me. It's someone else. Once the sound comes back and the blood rushing in my eyes dissipates, I hear it. It's my baby.

"You did it, Dove," Evander says, tears streaming down his face.

Thalia catches him with practiced grace and cradles him close.

"A fighter," she says, handing him up to me. "This one came out ready to rule. It's a boy."

She hands him to me and I hold him to my chest. Evander looks at the two of us like the world just ended and began again all at once.

"Julian," I whisper. "His name is Julian."

Evander presses a kiss to my forehead. I can feel it tremble. But Thalia isn't finished.

"We're halfway there, love," Thalia says.

The words don't land at first.

Halfway?

Evander stiffens beside me. I try to speak. "What do you mean halfway—?"

Another contraction hits me like a slap.

No. No. No.

"Thalia!" I snap. "Why didn't anyone tell me?"

Evander's eyes are wild now. I can't tell if he's horrified or delighted. Possibly both.

"There's another?" he says.

"Twin souls," Thalia nods. "Fate doesn't always follow a stable plan."

The next wave rises. Faster. Harder. My body feels like it's trying to fold in on itself.

"Almost there," Thalia says. "This boy is a fighter as well."

A rush of warmth plops on me. A gasp. Not from me.

This child doesn't cry.

He just looks up at us, blinking, steady as moonlight. I gather him to my chest beside Julian—two tiny weights, one burning, one still.

"Owen," I breathe. "His name is Owen."

Evander brushes a hand through their dark hair, stunned into silence.

"Twins," he finally says. "Of course."

"You're welcome," Thalia says dryly. "Now lie still, all of you. I'm not cleaning blood off the floor."

I can't even laugh. I don't think I could move if I tried.

My body is wrecked. My heart is wide open.

Julian has finally stopped crying—his head tucked under my chin, one tiny fist curled against my collarbone. Owen is still quiet, but his fingers are tangled in the fabric of my shift like he knows me.

Evander hasn't stopped looking at them.

He's kneeling beside the bed, arms braced on either side of me like he's still trying to shield us from something—though there's nothing left to fight. Just the four of us and this new shape of love.

"Are you crying?" I whisper.

He blinks. Looks at me. Looks at them.

"I don't know," he says. "Maybe."

I press my cheek against Julian's soft head. "You should be. We made something perfect."

His fingers brush over Owen's tiny back, and for once—just once—Evander Duvain has no reply.

Thalia finishes cleaning up and leaves the room. I barely notice anything, but the two bundles in my arms. Nothing matters. I don't listen as Theron and Selene come in or my parents. I don't even listen to Evander.

I'm too busy holding the future.

Up Next

Sexy as Sin: Vegas (The Shadow Brides Series, Book 1.5)

Frankie & Beckett are about to break every rule.
A fiery bartender. A privileged heir. One hotel caught in the crossfire.
Whiskey, wildflowers, and way too much temptation collide in a combustible mix that's anything but business as usual.
**WELCOME TO SEXY AS SIN: LAS VEGAS, where ambition
and passion always burn bright!**
Coming November 1, 2025
Preorder now: https://a.co/d/fnnyBU9

**Can't wait? More From The Devil's Bargain coming for
you soon.**

Unholy Vows

You met them in The Devil's Canvas. Selene & Theron's story is
coming soon...
December 1, 2025
Preorder Here: https://a.co/d/a0FxaI7

Up Next in The Devil's Bargain Series...

(Book Three – Sloth)
He's never been in a hurry for anything.
She's spent her whole life giving too much, too fast.
But Sloth isn't just about waiting.
It's about taking your time to destroy something beautiful.
Coming March 2026

Extended Epilogue

Did you love *Wicked Union*?

Don't miss the exclusive extended epilogue—set sixteen years later, when Evander finally shares the truth about soulmate bonds with his sons and nephews.

Sign up for my newsletter to get the exclusive Evander POV epilogue free: https://dl.bookfunnel.com/myuiwr1941

About The Author

Deliciously Dark, Beautifully Twisted

Sara McClaflin writes romance with feelings, flaws, and just the right amount of emotional damage. Her stories are character-driven, morally gray, and often ask one very important question: what if love was a little dangerous—and we liked it that way? After years of reading and reviewing books with too much angst, she finally started writing her own.

She lives on the West Coast with her husband, their chaotic dog, and more book boyfriends than she's willing to admit. Her TBR pile is a cry for help, her playlists are 80% heartbreak, and she's always chasing the next character who'll ruin her in the best way.

Newsletter Sign Up: https://subscribepage.io/saras-newsletter

amazon.com/stores/Sara-McClaflin/author/B0CR8VHBHJ?ref=ap
_rdr&isDramIntegrated=true&shoppingPortalEnabled=true&ccs_i
d=1fcaa1c2-62ac-4142-ab01-dce9c490e471

bookbub.com/profile/sara-mcclaflin

goodreads.com/author/show/47632250.Sara_McClaflin

instagram.com/authorsaramcclaflin/

facebook.com/profile.php?id=61551822185090&notif_id=174422
8205391402&notif_t=page_user_activity&ref=notif#

tiktok.com/@sara.mcclaflin

Also By

The Devil's Bargain

Wicked Union– A prequel novella (Liora and Evander's story)

The Devil's Canvas

Gilded Lies

The Shadow Brides

Veil of Fire

The Huntington Brothers Series

Destined for Love

Tangled Hearts

Promises to Keep

Standalone Novels

The Keeper's Secret

Love on the Edge

Anthologies

Head in the Clouds: A Romantic Comedy Anthology

Desperate: A Deadly Thriller Anthology

❧

Did you love Wicked Union?

If you enjoyed the story, I would be so grateful if you took a moment to leave a quick review. Thank you for reading, for your support, and for spending time with these characters. I can't wait for you to see what happens next!

www.ingramcontent.com/pod-product-compliance
Lightning Source LLC
Chambersburg PA
CBHW030235180626
46810CB00008B/3139